A Bullet for Mr. Texas

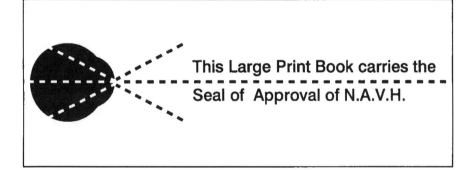

This Large Print Book carries the
Seal of Approval of N.A.V.H.

A Bullet for Mr. Texas

A Shawn Starbuck Western

Ray Hogan

G.K. Hall & Co. • **Thorndike, Maine**

Published in 1999 by arrangement with
Golden West Literary Agency.

G.K. Hall Large Print Western Series.

The text of this Large Print edition is unabridged.
Other aspects of the book may vary from the original edition.

Set in 16 pt. Plantin by Al Chase.

Printed in the United States on permanent paper.

Library of Congress Cataloging in Publication Data

Hogan, Ray, 1908–
    A bullet for Mr. Texas : a Shawn Starbuck western / by Ray Hogan.
    p.   cm.
    ISBN 0-7838-8613-6 (lg. print : hc : alk. paper)
    1. Large type books. I. Title. II. Title: Bullet for Mister Texas.
[PS3558.O3473B85 1999]
813′.54—dc21
                        99-14744

A Bullet for Mr. Texas

1

Shawn Starbuck wheeled lazily, hooked his elbows on the edge of the bar and glanced about the saloon. Except for two men at a corner table playing cutthroat poker, he was the sole patron. With his free hand he reached up, mopped at the sweat beading his face. The day was blistering hot — but no hotter than usual for July, he had been assured.

Taking a swallow of the cool beer he was holding, he shifted his gaze to the glare beyond the building's open doorway. The dusty street with its board sidewalks was also deserted. As was the custom in such Western towns, no one in Brasada was moving about at that hour of the day.

He sighed heavily. It had been a long haul from the Hebren Valley country. He had crossed some of the worst stretches of land in the state, and he was glad that it was all behind him. Not that he hadn't weathered tougher trails in his search for Ben, the brother who had run away from home ten years or so earlier, but unquestionably this had been the hottest.

It was done now, however. He had only to cover the twenty miles or so that yet remained and then he would reach Hagerman's Hash Knife ranch, his intended destination. Hopefully, he might find Ben there.

The quest for his brother, who had fled their Ohio farm home while still a boy in his mid-teens, following a turbulent scene with their father, was seemingly endless. It had taken him back and forth across the frontier in ceaseless fashion while he pursued various clues, ran down tips and investigated rumors that had come to him. So far his efforts had gone for naught; each time the person involved was clearly not Ben or else had moved on, leaving behind only the disturbing possibility that he might have been.

He could be facing disappointment once again at Hagerman's. That thought stirred him, caused him to shrug indifferently. He had grown accustomed to failure, had come to accept it philosophically, consider it a part of his way of life. He reckoned he could do little else, for his description of Ben, based on what he recalled of a boy now grown into a man ten years older than himself, was pitifully meager.

And the name — Ben Starbuck — had no meaning. His brother, in seething, departing anger, had declared he not only was leaving home for all time to come but was also ridding himself of the family name and thus slashing forevermore all connection with Hiram Starbuck. Thus, Shawn had little of a concrete nature to go on except the presence of a small scar above his brother's eye and a determination to one day find Ben, or proof of his death, and thereby settle old Hiram's estate and claim his own rightful share.

"You looking for company, cowboy?"

Shawn, pulled from his thoughts, turned to face the woman who had moved up next to him at the bar. She was yellow-haired, had heavily rouged lips and cheeks, and wore a gaudy red and gold dress that clung to her body. He had noticed her earlier leaning against the railing of the gallery that ran the width of the saloon's second floor.

"My name's Artha, and being company for lonesome cowpunchers is my business."

Starbuck grinned. It pulled down the corners of his eyes somewhat, reversed the studied gravity of his features and gave him an almost boyish look.

"Maybe I look it but I'm no more lonesome than usual. Just doing some thinking."

The woman brushed at a loose strand of hair straggling across her forehead, motioned to the man behind the bar. "Nate, I'll have a rye on my friend, here."

The bartender, a squat, red-faced man with a close cropped mustache, lifted his brows questioningly at Starbuck, reached for a bottle and glass when Shawn nodded. One of the men engaged in the two-handed poker game swore suddenly. His opponent laughed.

"Thinking," Artha said slowly. "Means you got yourself a girl somewheres and you're doing some wishing."

"No, it was about my brother. I'm here looking for him."

Artha took up her glass, tossed off half its contents in a single gulp. "He here in Brasada? Could be I know him."

"Not exactly sure he is."

"So . . . What's he look like?"

"Expect we sort of favor each other, but he'll probably be some heavier. Eyes will be blue, real light maybe. Hair'll be dark."

"Sounds like forty other jaspers I know," the woman said bluntly. "He got a name?"

"Ben Starbuck — but I doubt if he'll be using that."

"Then how the hell —"

"Good chance he calls himself Damon Friend."

Artha was quiet for a long minute while she swished the remainder of her drink about in the glass. Finally she shook her head. "Don't ring no bells. Seems to me you don't know much about him yourself."

"Been a long time since I saw him — ten years and a bit more. We were only kids then." Shawn turned to the bartender hovering closeby and listening. "You think maybe you've seen him?"

Nate, the bartender, brushed the sweat off his face. "Hard to say. Ain't much of a description, and there's a lot of men riding through nowadays."

"He could have put on a boxing exhibition. Did in the last town where I managed to track him."

"Boxing . . . You mean that fancy kind of fighting, like that man on the belt buckle you're wearing?"

Shawn nodded. "He's put on matches to raise money a couple of times that I know of. Might have done it here."

Nate stroked his mustache, stared at the card players. "No, sure don't recollect no such a exhibition, as you call it. You a fighter, too?"

"Pa taught us both how to take care of ourselves. He was an expert at it — could have been a champion, I guess, had he wanted. Buckle belonged to him. Came to me when he died."

"What made you think this Ben would be here in Brasada?" Artha asked, downing the rest of her liquor.

"Not exactly here that I was expecting to find him. Got a tip that a man sort of answering the right description worked for a rancher named Hagerman — the Hash Knife outfit. You know where it is from here?"

"Know!" Nate echoed. "Hagerman's the reason there's a town!"

"Big spread, that it?" Starbuck's hopes rose a notch. A ranch with a large number of hired hands always presented good possibilities.

"Big ain't the word for it," Artha said caustically. "Two hundred thousand acres and Price Hagerman's working for the day when he'll have a steer standing on every last one. He'll make it, too, if he don't run out of meanness and bullets — which ain't likely."

11

"Easy, now," Nate murmured. "Long as there's Hagerman's, we're in business."

The woman shrugged. "If there wasn't, I'd just go somewheres else. Hagerman ain't got no lease on my life. Pulls on his pants same way as any other man does."

Nate winked broadly at Starbuck. "And I reckon you sure ought to know, Artha," he said, slyly.

Her shoulders twitched again, gently rippling the smooth skin under its thin covering. "His money's good as the next jasper's . . . You think your brother's working for him?"

"What I hope."

"Well, guess he could be. I don't know all the hands on Hash Knife — must be fifty, maybe sixty of them. And there's a couple other saloons in town. Some go there. All this talking — it worth another drink to you?"

Shawn bobbed his head at Nate, leaned back against the long counter. He was a tall man, running to leanness, with dark hair that tended to curl along his neck when it was in need of trimming, as it was now. His brows were thick, overhung gray-blue eyes that appeared almost colorless in the shadowy lamplight. He seemed much older than his actual years, for the change had been sudden and it had taken but a short time for the hard way of life common to the frontier to convert the raw farm boy into a cool-nerved trail rider adept not only in the ordinary trades of the time but also in the science of

12

staying alive in a world of violence where only the quick and the skilled moved safely.

"Hoping you won't go carrying tales about what Artha said." Nate's voice was hesitant, was burdened with a thread of worry. "She don't mean nothing by it."

"Stops with me," Starbuck answered. "If this Hagerman's big as you claim, doubt if he ever pays much attention to what folks say about him, anyway."

"You can just bet he don't!" the woman declared. "He likes it. Makes him feel taller. There's some who even call him Mr. Texas!"

Shawn grinned at her. "Maybe it fits."

"He likes to think it does, but there's those who don't —"

"Never mind now, Artha," Nate broke in. "Don't go getting too wise."

"Somebody like him having enemies, that's not new," Shawn said, coming about and placing his empty mug on the bar. "Any time a man gets busy and makes something big of himself there's always a few ready to start sniping at him."

"A few, maybe, but it ain't usual for everybody to be doing it — even their own flesh and blood!" the woman snapped.

Nate's palm came down hard on the counter. "That's aplenty now, Artha! You've shot off your mouth enough."

"His own kids — Ron and that Rhoda — they hate him like poison!"

"You don't know that," the barman said.

"You're only guessing."

"Don't have to guess. I been with Ron more'n once and I've listened to him bitch. Anyway, you can easy see it in them — way they act." Artha paused long enough to drain her glass. "Know what? I got a feeling he hates them bad as they do him!"

Starbuck rubbed at the stubble on his chin. "Sounds like quite a family. Where does the mother fit?"

"She's dead — since the boy and his sister were only buttons, I've heard tell," Nate said. "All live in a big, fancy house with a Mexican woman doing the cooking and housekeeping."

"Explains a lot," Starbuck said idly. "Having a mother around makes a lot of difference. Always sort of keeps things in balance."

He was thinking of his own mother, Clare, in that moment. Matters had gone smoothly for the Starbuck family while she lived. A quiet, intelligent woman who had been a school teacher prior to marriage, she had been the buffer that stood firmly between her iron-fisted husband and their two sons. In a little more than a year after her death from lung fever, Ben had gone.

He wiped at the moisture on his jaw. "Well, I don't expect to have any truck with your Mr. Texas and his kin, only with his hired help." Reaching into a pocket, he added: "How much I owe you?"

"Dollar'll cover it all — your beer and Artha's rye."

Shawn dropped the coin on the counter. "How's the best way to get to Hash Knife?"

Nate had drawn up slowly, was looking toward the saloon's entrance, a frown pulling at his features. An elderly man wearing knee high, flat heeled Hyer boots, with corded pants tucked into them, a white shirt with string tie, and a flat crowned hat was coming into the room. He carried cross-belted guns and there was a star pinned to his chest.

"That's Ira Blackburn, the marshal," Nate said in a low voice. "Looks like he's got something on his mind."

2

The lawman's eyes, flat and filled with hostility, were on Starbuck. The tall rider sighed quietly. He had encountered that look before — one reserved for unwelcome drifters and suspected outlaws — and recognized in it the promise of trouble.

"He's probably thinking you're the jaybird who's supposed to have a bullet for Price Hagerman," Artha murmured. "Figures every stranger that rides into town is the man."

Shawn watched Blackburn pull to a stop an arm's reach away. The old lawman's persimmon face was frozen. His mustache bristled.

"Don't recollect seeing you around here before," he said.

"First time," Starbuck replied.

"You got a name?"

"Starbuck . . . Shawn Starbuck."

The poker game in the corner of the saloon had come to a halt, both men now standing to get a better look at the proceedings. Nate, features expressionless, was leaning against the back bar.

"Mind telling me what you're doing in my town?"

Shawn shifted irritably. He had nothing to hide but such confrontations always evoked a glow of anger within him. Some lawmen seemed to think they owned the town they represented and were privileged to challenge any and all who entered their precincts.

"Looking for his brother," Artha said, taking it upon herself to make a reply. "Figures he works for Hagerman."

Blackburn crossed his arms, the belligerence in him growing stronger. He considered Starbuck through narrowed eyes. "That so?"

"The way it is."

"Brother's name is Ben — or maybe he's calling himself Damon Friend. He's a fighter — a boxer, or whatever you call them fancy kind. Was asking if he could've put on a show here."

Shawn flicked the woman with an annoyed glance. Such details he had not intended for the lawman — or any lawman — to hear. Ben was wanted for murder in New Mexico Territory and information on him described him as a skilled boxer who likely staged exhibitions of the art.

"A boxer, eh?" Blackburn murmured, expression still unchanging. "What makes you think he's at Hagerman's? Never heard no mention of them names, neither one."

"Word came to me," Shawn replied, relieved that Artha's revelation had raised no special interest in the old lawman. Either the New Mexico sheriff had not forwarded details of the charge standing against Ben this far east or Blackburn had simply forgotten.

"Where you hail from?"

"About any place you'd care to mention. Been looking for my brother for some time and every once in a while I have to stop, find myself a job and raise some cash. Sort of makes me a citizen of quite a few —"

"I'm talking about your home — where you come from at the beginning."

"Ohio. Town called Muskingum. My folks had a farm along the river."

"You prove that?"

Impatience moved Starbuck. "I need to?" he asked in a level voice.

For a first time there was a relenting in Ira Blackburn's contentious attitude. He raised his left hand slowly, carefully, brushed his hat to the back of his head and wiped at the sweat collected on his brow.

"No, reckon not — leastwise for the time being. Can't see no call for you traipsing out to Hagerman's, however. Like I said, there ain't nobody out there by them names, far as I know."

"Best I see for myself, Marshal."

"Why?" Hostility rose again in the lawman. "Ain't my telling you enough?"

"Not that. Happens I'm the only one who can recognize him. Not sure what he looks like, and he could be going under some name other than the ones I mentioned."

"Meaning you don't know what he calls himself or what he looks like?"

"About the size of it."

"Then how the hell you expect to ever find him?"

"Only one sure way. There's a scar over his left eye. Hid mostly by the brow, but it's there. One thing for sure I can go by."

Ira Blackburn shrugged, cocked his head to one side. "Know what I'm thinking, mister?"

"I can guess," Shawn replied indifferently. "It won't change a thing. Whether you believe me or not, it's the truth — and I'm riding out to Hagerman's place."

Again the marshal brushed at his forehead. "Well, there ain't no lawful way I can stop you, but if you want some good advice, forget it."

"Can't. Rode across a lot of country getting here. Not about to move on until I do what I came for."

Blackburn stared at Starbuck for a long breath and then, with a slight twitch of his shoulders, said, "Suit yourself," pivoted and marched stiffly out of the saloon.

Artha laughed derisively. "There goes the toughest lawman in Texas!"

"Was once," Nate said, shaking his head at her. "Was a time when he walked plenty tall — Abilene, Wichita, San Antone and the like. Wore a star right along with the best of them."

"Like you said — there was a time," the woman drawled, tucking the wisp of stray hair back into place again. "That ain't now. He's an old man, wore out . . . and living on what he used to be. The real law around here is our high and

19

mighty Mr. Texas — and you know it."

Nate smiled thinly. "Sure I know it — and so does Ira Blackburn. Which makes it all come out even, far as I can see." He shifted his attention to Shawn. "Ain't that the way it looks to you?"

"Don't ring me in on it," Starbuck said with a laugh. "I'm just passing through. Fact is, I'm moving on right now — for Hagerman's. How do I get there?"

"Take the road east out of town, and keep riding. You'll come to a post. There's a board on it with Hagerman's brand burned into it — the Hash Knife."

"Ought to be a skull and crossbones," Artha observed acidly.

"It's the way he marks his range boundary. Got them posts around the place ever so often. Anyways, when you get to the marker, you're about five miles from the ranch. Can spot it easy. Big layout built at the edge of a grove."

Shawn nodded, took a step away from the bar. He was thinking about something the woman had said, and its evident relation to Blackburn's attitude.

"There really somebody out to kill Hagerman — or was that just talk?"

Nate picked up Starbuck's empty beer mug, began to scrub at the ring of moisture it had left. He slid a glance at the two men at the table. They had resumed their poker game.

"Word's out that a killer's been hired to gun him down."

"Who's behind it?"

"Ain't nobody knows who. Lot of folks would like to see him dead, which sure ain't no secret. He stepped on a lot of corns getting where he is."

"Maybe most people don't know who but I can give you a close guess —"

"Never mind, Artha," the bartender cut in sternly. "Just you keep your guessing to yourself. One of these days your lip's going to get you in a lot of trouble!"

The woman sniffed, jerked her head perfunctorily.

Shawn grinned at her, at Nate.

"Obliged to you both. Expect I'll be seeing you later," he said and moved for the doorway.

3

Starbuck stepped out onto the saloon's gallery, feeling the blast of heat as he faced the glare, and crossed to the hitchrack where his horse waited.

The sorrel was a fairly new mount to him. When he had ridden away from the Hebren Valley he had been astride a black that had belonged to an outlaw. Fearing the animal had been stolen, he handed it over to the first lawman he encountered and bought himself a mount he could ride without being afraid of getting himself strung up somewhere along the line as a horsethief.

Jerking the sorrel's reins free, he looped them back about the animal's long neck and swung onto the saddle. The leather was cook-stove hot. He flinched, swore softly and eased himself forward.

Glancing up to the front of the saloon, he read the aging sign nailed to its high front — THE CHINABERRY — assumed again that it took its name from the tall tree that grew alongside and cast its shade over the structure.

All was still quiet in Brasada, it appeared. He did note, however, two women who had braved the heat and were now standing under the porch roof of Peyton's General Store at the end of the dusty lane engaged in earnest conversation. But no other person was in sight and the settlement, to all intents, was deserted — a ghost town of weathered buildings with sagging facades, streaky windows and a small, lonely church with a white steeple standing apart in an empty field.

He eased back into the saddle, found it now acceptable, and settled in comfortably. Motion in the doorway of The Chinaberry caught his eye as he cut the sorrel about. It was Artha. She had followed him to the entrance, stood with a hand raised in a farewell, a strange, stilled look on her painted face. From that distance her features appeared artificial and doll-like.

Shawn touched the brim of his hat and rode on, guiding the gelding into the middle of the street and pointing him for the road that struck eastward. When he passed the marshal's office he gave it casual notice. The lawman's quarters were empty, the door closed.

After what Artha and Nate had told him of the threat hanging over Price Hagerman, he had a better understanding of Blackburn's attitude toward him. Any stranger riding into Brasada would be suspect. He reckoned if he'd been wearing the star he would have reacted in the same manner.

Hagerman would be a hard man to protect, he guessed, judging from what he had heard of the rancher, and he would have a legion of well earned enemies. He certainly didn't envy Ira Blackburn his job.

Reaching the end of the street, Shawn veered

the sorrel onto the right hand fork, casually noting as he did the distant, towering mountain peaks. All looked hazy and remote in the bright heat. The visible signs of a hot summer were everywhere — gray-brown grass thin as smoke, drooping chamisa, dusty trees; even the globular snakeweed, or turpentine bush as he'd heard it called in the area, seemed to be wilted.

He would try to avoid Price Hagerman, he decided. The son and daughter as well, if it was at all possible. From the sound of things and the hints that had lain in the words spoken by Artha and Nate, the Hagermans were a family best kept at a distance. There should really be no reason to encounter them. The foreman of Hash Knife was the logical man to seek out and put his questions to. In the past such had always proved the most effective plan.

He hadn't remembered to ask the name of the foreman when he was in The Chinaberry. . . . No matter. . . . Somewhere along the way he'd undoubtedly run into one of Hagerman's hired hands. He'd find out then.

Reaching up, he removed his hat, forearmed the sweat from his features. He could have stalled out a couple or more hours back in the saloon, waited for a cooler time to ride, but it hadn't occurred to him. He shrugged. If it had he likely would have ruled against it. Whenever he was close to finding out something about Ben, an urgency within him pushed relentlessly, forced him to press on until he had the answer to

24

his question, knew whether the object of his visit was his brother or not.

The possibility that he would find Ben at Hash Knife didn't sound promising — if he were to draw conclusions from what Artha and Nate told him. They had given him no reason for hope at all and it seemed likely they should know, as Ben unquestionably would be at least an occasional patron of The Chinaberry.

As was always the trouble, he had so little to go on, so inadequate a description to give. And as for a name — Ben could be calling himself almost anything. That he had used Damon Friend was a certainty, but there was nothing to say he could not have dropped that for another. Such would be a sure bet if he had become aware of the fact that he was wanted in New Mexico under that name — for murder.

It had been more or less an accident, the sheriff had told Shawn, but it was a matter that would require Ben's presence to clear it up. Starbuck had been fairly sure there would be certain circumstances surrounding the killing; Ben had been hot-headed and strong willed, but being a murderer was not in him.

At least Shawn didn't think so. Every now and then he had to pause, however, and remind himself that the Ben of today was likely much changed from the Ben who had stalked out of the yard in Muskingum after a severe thrashing at the hands of old Hiram ten long years ago.

He could have hardened, become calloused, a

far cry from the son of Clare and the brother he had known. But he expected change, and thus anticipating it made the search all the more difficult. It was as if he sought a stranger, and likely, when he found Ben, he would be a stranger.

If he found him.

Shawn shifted wearily on the saddle as he gave that thought. There was no *if* to it; he must find Ben, or absolute proof of his death, otherwise the small fortune and all hope of the future he envisioned for himself was lost. But could he pursue the search forever, become a penniless drifter, gradually aging, accumulating little other than experience? It was like chasing a rainbow and —

Starbuck drew in the sorrel abruptly. The hard beat of a running horse somewhere behind him was like a hollow throb on the still air. It was a hot day for a man to gallop his mount, he thought, and immediately wondered why. At once he cut off the road and crossed quickly to a clump of tall brush pocketed in a shallow coulee.

Insects, hushed by his sudden approach, resumed their clacking. High overhead half a dozen buzzards, undisturbed by the movements of men, continued their slow, lowering circles, intent upon something that exhibited no motion well back in the hills.

Ignoring the harsh drive of the sun, Shawn fixed his eyes on the road. The rider, whoever he was, would first appear on the crest of a rise and then drop down into the broad swale he was presently crossing. He would be in view for a considerable distance.

At that moment the horseman broke into sight. Starbuck smiled grimly. At was Ira Blackburn. The lawman was bent forward on his saddle, sunlight glittering off his badge as he stared ahead.

At once he straightened, began to slacken the pace of the long-legged bay he was straddling. Features puzzled, he passed the brush where Shawn waited. It was evident he was searching for someone on the road.

It was for him, Starbuck realized. Blackburn had followed him from town at a distance, planning, no doubt, to keep an eye on him. The old marshal was still unconvinced that he was not the man sent to kill Price Hagerman.

Shawn smiled again, waited out the time until Blackburn had topped out the far edge of the swale and then returned to the road. Temper had risen within him. He didn't enjoy the idea of being a suspected killer and of having a lawman dogging his tracks — and then he recalled his previous thoughts on the matter and guessed Blackburn should be excused for his zealousness.

When he reached the lower end of the hollow, he threw his glance as far down the dusty strip of trail as he could. There was no sign of the lawman, but the road now curved somewhat to the south and trees were becoming evident. It was likely Blackburn had disappeared into one of the small clusters or was hidden behind a bend.

Not far ahead he caught a glimpse of a post with a sign fastened to it, reckoned it was the marker Nate had mentioned. Halting before it he considered the insignia burned into the soft wood with a branding iron. A hash knife with a circle — therefore, the Circle Hash Knife. Apparently nobody bothered to quote the full brand, only the Hash Knife part.

It was a good way to declare a boundary, Starbuck thought, and rode on, smiling as he remembered what Artha had said the true marking should be.

In the distance he saw the broad patch of dark green that would be the grove where Hagerman had built his ranch houses. A fairly large slash of silver marked the presence of a river, and below it three smaller and widely separated ribbons indicated lesser creeks. Well beyond it all a high peak loomed up against the steel blue of the sky.

It would appear that Hagerman had placed his house and buildings at the upper edge of his range and had a mountain of his own in his backyard. It seemed fitting; a man such as Price Hagerman — Mr. Texas — could be expected to have a personal monument of towering grandeur.

The road descended fairly rapidly, the long slope slicing in and out patches of trees to fade, finally into the grove itself. It should be a lot cooler in the deep shade, Shawn thought as the sorrel entered the fringe. It would be a welcome change. It seemed to him he'd known nothing but blasting, withering heat from the day he'd ridden from the Rio Grande and —

The sorrel's head came up sharply. He shied wildly to one side, catching Starbuck unawares, almost unseating him.

"Hold it right there!"

Anger rocked through Shawn as the hard edged words lashed at him. His hand, resting on the butt of the forty-five slung against his left hip, hung motionless for a long moment and then drifted slowly away as he looked into the muzzle of a pistol leveled at him. It was Marshal Ira Blackburn.

4

The corners of Starbuck's jaw whitened as he fought to curb the anger swelling within him. The lawman was allowing his sense of duty to carry him away.

"What the hell's eating you, Marshal?" he demanded, raising his arms slowly. "You know damned well I —"

"I don't know nothing about you for sure, but I got me one mighty big hunch," Blackburn cut in quietly. "Keep them hands up high."

Sweat glistening on his face, the older man kneed his horse around, approached Shawn from the rear. Abruptly he jammed the muzzle of his weapon into Starbuck's side. Then, reaching out, he lifted the tall rider's pistol from its holster and pulled back.

"What I told you was the truth."

"We'll see," Blackburn replied, thrusting Shawn's forty-five under his waistband. "For my money, I'm saying you're the killer we been looking for."

Starbuck shook his head in exasperation. "And for mine, you're loco — a plain fool."

"Maybe . . . Move out."

Shawn had a quick recollection of the marshal's small office and its accompanying jail back in Brasada. It would be like frying in Hades.

"No —"

Blackburn's thumb drew back the tall hammer of the heavy caliber pistol he was holding. He waggled it promisingly.

"Don't fret me, son. Just you head out for Hagerman's. Aim to let him see you, tell me what I ought to do."

Starbuck shrugged. That was better than being locked up — and if he could talk with Hagerman there was a good chance he could make the rancher see reason. Nobody could be as thick skulled as Ira Blackburn. Roweling the sorrel gently, he started the big gelding down the road.

"Yarn you're a-telling is pretty thin," the lawman said conversationally after they were under way. "Got to studying on it. Plain didn't make no sense."

"It's the truth," Shawn said in a patient voice. "Every last word of it."

"Yeh — looking for a brother that you don't know what he looks like or even what his name is. . . . A crock of bull if ever I —"

"Easy to prove. There a telegraph office around close?"

"Nope, not this side of San Angelo. Won't be needing one anyway."

"Seems I'm needing something to prove what I say."

"It'll be up to Hagerman. Aim to let him handle it."

Shawn fell silent. It was useless to argue with the old lawman. His best chance for straightening out matters would lie with the rancher. Likely, Price Hagerman, despite the things he'd heard about him, would prove to be a reasonable man.

They continued on, now following a fairly good road that cut a direct line through the grove. It was pleasant in the shade and it would have been an agreeable passage under other circumstances.

A short time later they left the trees and came onto the flat where Hagerman's ranch stood. Shawn stirred with admiration as he looked at the place — one much finer than he had expected to see. The house, a two-storied frame with a wide verandah and boasting large columns, was painted a clean white and reminded him of some of the homes he'd seen in the country of the lower Mississippi.

It was well protected by tall elms and sycamores with a scattering of cottonwoods and chinaberrys. There were also several gingkos in evidence, all loaded with pale orange fruit. Beds of flowers bordered the porch and the windows of the ground floor were vivid with potted geraniums. A creek sparkled in the sunlight a short distance away.

There were a number of buildings on the far side of the clearing — barns, sheds, bunkhouses, a roofed lean-to under which carriages had been rolled. Beyond all this was a maze of corrals and holding pens. Strangely, there was no one to be seen, only a solitary horse standing at a hitchrack fronting a squat adobe hut to the right of the main house.

Likely it had been Hagerman's original ranchhouse, Shawn thought.

"Pull up over there," Blackburn ordered, pointing at the rack. "Hagerman'll be in his office."

Shawn veered the gelding in next to the dozing buckskin, waited. The lawman moved in beside him, careful to keep his distance, and came stiffly off the saddle.

"All right, climb off."

A door slapped loudly into the hot silence as Starbuck swung from the sorrel. He turned, looked toward the main house. A girl of about his own age, dark hair, full brows to match and with deep blue eyes was coming toward them. There was a strong beauty to her features, and the tight, bright yellow shirt, open at the neck, and the corded skirt she was wearing brought out the finer points of her figure to a planned perfection.... Hagerman's daughter, no doubt.

She smiled at Blackburn, glanced at Shawn curiously. "Who's this, Marshal?"

"Howdy, Miss Rhoda," the lawman answered. "Brought him out to see your pa. Says his name is Starbuck. I've got a feeling he's the bird we've been watching out for."

A stillness came over the girl as she considered Shawn more deliberately. "You mean he's the —"

"The marshal's wrong," Starbuck cut in flatly.

"I came here looking for my brother."

"That's what set me onto him — crazy story he's telling about hunting a brother. No sense to it a'tall."

Rhoda Hagerman moved up nearer to Starbuck. Her eyes, he noted, were so deep a blue as to be almost black. Despite the intense heat she appeared cool and there was a faint fragrance of perfume to her. Shawn grinned at the frank appraisal she gave him.

"It's just the way I've told him, lady. . . . I don't know anything about your pa — never heard of him before, in fact. And I sure didn't come here to shoot him."

"You don't look like a killer — or sound like one either."

Blackburn snorted his derision at her womanly logic. "How's a killer supposed to look and talk?"

Rhoda shrugged. "Not like him, I'll bet on that."

"Well, we'll let your pa decide. He around?"

The girl smiled wryly, nodded at the adobe hut. "All you need do is listen and you've got the answer to that."

Shawn turned his attention to the small structure. From its thick walled interior he could hear the muffled sound of a deep voice rising and falling.

"He's got Dave Archer in there," Rhoda said. "Been giving him holy hell for the last half hour over something."

Blackburn listened for a long minute, seemingly undecided as to whether he should interrupt or not. He ran his finger around the inside of his collar, cleared his throat.

"There been trouble or something going on?"

"No more than usual," the girl answered. "Rustling, of course. Never stops. Hired help quitting or getting hurt, stock foundering in the quicksand along the San Fernando and getting lost in the brakes — things like that. . . . Every time we lose a steer you can hear him hollering all the way to Mexico. You'd think his life depended on one flea-bit cow."

Blackburn nodded woodenly and continued to stare in the direction of the hut. "Well, maybe I'd best take this fellow back to town," he said hesitantly. "I'll lock him up and your pa can ride in —"

"No sense in that," Rhoda said, shrugging. "Just go right on in. He'll be through dressing down Dave in a few more minutes. Ron's inside there, too, waiting for him."

"You figure it'd be all right?"

"Of course it will. I'll even go with you. I've a feeling I ought to be there."

Ira Blackburn made no reply. He gave it all a few moments additional thought and then jabbing Shawn with his pistol, jerked his head toward the hut.

"Let's go," he said almost reluctantly. "And you'd best mind your manners."

5

They crossed the narrow distance that separated the rack from the hut. With each step the thunder of Price Hagerman's voice increased in volume, and as Rhoda, slightly ahead of Shawn and the marshal, opened the door and entered, she gave the tall rider a half smile.

"Welcome to the lion's den," she murmured.

The hut had two rooms, the first now serving as a sort of waiting or lobby area while Hagerman conducted business in the one adjoining which was cut off by a connecting slab door.

Shawn, eyes adjusting slowly to the abrupt change from brilliant sunlight to deep shade, halted in the center of the small cubicle. The barrel of Blackburn's pistol was pressing into his back and he turned to the old lawman, frowning.

"You don't need that," he said impatiently and stepped away, noting then the man lounging against the wall.

He would be Hagerman's son — Ron. A slender, dark man with eyes like Rhoda's. He appeared to be a few years older. Shawn nodded slightly to him.

Hagerman returned the greeting coolly. There was a reserved quality to him, a withdrawal that was almost a fear. He'd been a target all too often for his father's wrath; such was easy to see.

"I don't give a good goddam who it was! You're the foreman around here!"

Price Hagerman's words hammered through the intervening door and wall. Rhoda smiled wanly again, shook her head. Ron stirred, shifted his weight from left leg to right, ducked his head at Shawn.

"Who's he?"

"A gunman, so the marshal thinks," Rhoda replied, studying her brother intently as she spoke. "Figures he's the one that was coming to kill Pa."

Ron Hagerman straightened. His mouth tightened into a tight line.

"What makes you think that, Ira?"

"Several things — stranger . . . just blew into town. Gun he's wearing shows a lot of use. Trigger spring's been honed down."

"Not much to go on."

"Ain't just that, he —"

"Bottom dollar on them steers'd be eighteen dollars a head!" Price Hagerman's outraged voice again filled the small room. "Eighteen goddam dollars, hear? That's better'n two hundred for the twelve you lost!"

"Ain't just that," Blackburn said again when the rancher's tones had once more lapsed to a low grumble. "Tells me some fool tale about a brother he's hunting that makes no sense."

Ron's brows lifted questioningly at Starbuck. Shawn only shrugged, seeing no point in going into details again. As well wait and do his explaining where it would count — to Price Hagerman.

Blackburn glanced nervously at the closed door. "Think your pa'll be much longer? I could come back later."

"Expect he's about through with Archer," Ron answered, resuming his position against the wall. "Been roasting him now for —"

"I ain't taking the loss — I'll tell you that right now, Dave! You're paid good, hard money to look after my beef — something I expect you to do!"

Archer's voice finally lifted to a point where the sound of it could be heard, but his words were still unintelligible.

"The hell! Proves nothing! Now here's the way it's going to be! I'm taking no loss, like I said. You're working the next two months for nothing — paying off for them steers! Understand? Two months' wages'll just about cover what them steers was worth. You got it straight?"

Archer made some sort of reply.

"All right then — get yourself back on the job, and, by God, I'd better not lose no more stock or else —" The inner door jerked open. Dave Archer, a man of middle age with a sun and windburned, craggy face, stepped into the room. Eyes burning, ignoring all those waiting, he crossed to the screen, elbowed it aside and stalked rigidly to his waiting horse.

"All right, what do you want?"

At Hagerman's roughly put question, Shawn turned to the rancher. Blackburn, who had been watching Dave Archer's ignominious departure also, came about hastily.

"Like to see you a minute, Price — was you not too busy," he stammered.

Hagerman's bristling bulk filled the doorway. He wore a full mustache peppered black and gray as was the thick shock that crowned his head. His face appeared as a series of horizontal lines — square cut chin, slash mouth, hedgerow brows and straight across hairline. His eyes were small, piercing, seemed colorless in their deep sockets. His offspring took more from their mother in both appearance and mannerisms, it would seem.

"What're you hanging around for?" he demanded, ignoring Blackburn and fixing his gaze on Ron. "You know the rule — nobody's to be on the place while there's work to be done."

"Which is all the time," Rhoda observed lightly.

The rancher swung his glance to her. "We can do without your lip, missy," he snapped, and again turned to his son. "I asked you a question. Seems I recollect telling you to ride down to the Cow Creek pond, get that branding finished up. You fall down on that, too?"

"No, Pa," Ron said wearily. "It was all done when I got there. I came back to see what else you wanted me to do."

"Goddammit!" Hagerman exploded. "I got

two hundred thousand acres with forty thousand cows running on it and you can't find yourself something to do! You sure you don't want me blowing your nose for you?"

Ron stirred in a helpless sort of way and looked down. "Well, I thought maybe —"

"Hell, don't bother thinking! Only get you in a mess, same as it always has. If you can't find nothing better to do, get on down to the stable, fork manure. Ought to be a job you can handle with no trouble."

Ron Hagerman's face crimsoned. He shook his head, drew away from the wall.

"Now, what're you doing here, Blackburn, and who's this jasper with you?"

The lawman came up with a start. "Stranger I seen riding in and figured —"

"You want something?" Hagerman broke in, attention now centering on his daughter as he once again ignored the marshal.

Rhoda smiled, arched her brows. "Just listening. Just go right ahead — don't worry about me."

"I never do," the rancher snapped. "Not that it would do me any good."

"That's right, Pa," the girl said with exaggerated sweetness.

"All right, Blackburn — talk up! What do you want? I've got work to do — have to depend on myself for everything around the damned place. Can't bank on nobody, not even my own foreman. Let me lose twelve prime steers out of

40

pure carelessness — and me paying him higher wages than he could get from any other outfit in the country! Spit it out, Ira — what're you after?"

"He's been trying to tell you, Pa," Rhoda said, "but you won't give him a chance. He thinks he's caught the would-be killer."

Price Hagerman drew himself up to his full height. His eyes narrowed. "That right?"

"Pretty sure of it," Blackburn said. "Stranger that just rode in. Telling a crazy yarn about hunting a brother."

The rancher moved into the room, pulled up close to Starbuck, stared hard at him. His broad face was stolid.

"So you're the sonofabitch that's come to put a bullet in me —"

Shawn's knotted fist smashed into Hagerman's jaw, drove him back a step. A small cry burst from Rhoda's lips as Hagerman's hand swept down for the pistol on his hip, paused as Blackburn jammed his own weapon into Starbuck's spine.

Shawn, glowing with anger, faced the rancher. "Nobody calls me that — not you or anybody else," he said coldly.

Hagerman, fingers probing tenderly the area along his chin, considered Starbuck thoughtfully. A ghost of a smile tugged at Ron's lips and a light had come alive in Rhoda's dark eyes.

Blackburn locked his fingers around Shawn's wrist with his free hand, pressed harder with the pistol clenched in the other.

"You want me to take him in, lock him up, Price?" he asked worriedly. He was blaming himself for his carelessness — and dreading the consequence.

Hagerman wagged his head slowly. "Forget it. I'll take care of him."

The lawman frowned. "Ain't it something for the law to —"

"Said I'd handle it!" the rancher barked. "That his gun you've got stuck in your pants?" he added, pointing.

Blackburn pulled Shawn's weapon from his waistband, passed it to Hagerman. "Well, if that's how you're wanting it, Price."

"It's how I want it. Now, get on your way. Maybe you can scare yourself up a couple of drunks on the way back to town."

Ira Blackburn made no reply, simply wheeled about and moved toward the door. The rancher glanced to Ron.

"What the hell you still doing here? Told you to start working."

The younger Hagerman immediately swung in behind the lawman, trailed him out into the yard.

"Believe I'll stay," Rhoda announced brightly as her parent's attention swung to her.

"You will like hell! Get out of here, find something to do."

"Like what?"

"How the devil would I know? What are girls

who're letting themselves turn into old maids supposed to do? Knit . . . cook . . . make things —"

"Such as babies?"

Hagerman's eyes flashed. "Dammit — don't give me any of your cute lip! I won't stand for it. I raised you decent, and, by God, you're going to stay decent or —"

"Or?"

"Get out of here!" the rancher roared in exasperation, and took a long stride toward her.

Rhoda smiled, backed for the doorway. Reaching it she paused, gaze on Shawn. "I hope I'll be seeing you later, Mr. Starbuck. I'd like to get better acquainted."

Shawn nodded, amused by the girl's independence. "Like as not I'll be around."

"Fine," she murmured and stepped out into the sunlight.

Price Hagerman stared after her. He shrugged helplessly. "Hussy — acts like a regular hussy. Don't know how she comes by it." His words broke off suddenly as if abruptly aware he had been speaking aloud. The hardness came again into his features as he settled his eyes on Starbuck.

"All right," he said, pointing into the other room. "Get in there and set down. Want to know who you are and what brought you here if it ain't to put a bullet in me."

43

6

"You've been told," Shawn said indifferently, moving into the rancher's office.

The room was plainly furnished — a table that served as a desk now littered with papers; a chair behind it, two more placed to face it, a lamp. The walls were bare except for a smudged calendar that bore a lithographed reproduction of Abraham Lincoln.

Hagerman eased himself into his seat. Laying Shawn's pistol on top of the clutter before him, he motioned the tall rider to one of the chairs.

"Might as well set. Makes talking some easier," he said in a conciliatory tone.

Starbuck's shoulders twisted indifferently. He drew one of the chairs near, dropped into it, feeling the rancher's small eyes drilling into him.

"This brother you're hunting, what makes you think you'll find him here?"

Shawn's mouth parted into a small smile. "That mean you don't figure I'm the killer?"

"Not made up mind yet. Answer my question."

"I was told a man answering the description I gave of him worked for you."

"That so? What's he look like and what does he call himself?"

Starbuck went through the details he custom-

44

arily outlined. When he had concluded Price Hagerman stared at him from hooded eyes.

"Mighty thin, all right," he said finally. "I can see why the marshal got all worked up. But I reckon I can believe it."

"Suit yourself," Shawn said, settling back.

The rancher grunted. "You're a mite proddy, seems to me."

"It's the people I come up against. . . . You think you maybe've got somebody answering the description riding for you?"

"Hell, I don't know! I got fifty men working on this ranch and don't know a third of them — less'n that by name."

Starbuck rose, stepped to the lone window in the adjacent wall and peered out. "Must make it hard to tell the rustlers from the hired hands," he said dryly, eyes on two horsemen loping in from the direction of the mountain.

Hagerman laughed. "By God, that's a good one," he said, "and I reckon it's the truth. You know, I'm taking a shine to you. It real important you find this brother of yours?"

"Plenty," Shawn said, coming back around. "My pa died about a year after Ben ran off. Left everything to us, but before I can get my share I've got to find him, take him back to Muskingum or else have proof that he's dead. Otherwise I lose it all."

The rancher shifted, sighed deeply. "I see. . . . Doing some judging, I'd say you was a cut above the usual. Got some education under your hat.

45

Your pa responsible for that?"

"My mother. She was a fine woman. Been a school teacher before she married, saw to it Ben and I got a little more than our share of learning. Pa was a farmer. About all we got from him was how to box — fight with our fists."

"And be an honest to God man," Hagerman added, a faint thread of wistfulness in his voice. "You win that belt buckle you're wearing fighting?"

"No, it was Pa's. He used to put on exhibition matches when I was a kid. Neighbors all got together, presented it to him."

"He a champion?"

"Could have been, I guess, had he wanted, but he was more taken by farming — and to my mother. She meant everything to him. He was never the same after she died."

Hagerman's eyes were on his big hamlike hands lying clenched before him on the table. The knuckles shone whitely.

"I understand that. A woman can be everything to a man — the sum total of what he is, what he aims to be . . . My wife — Eunice — she passed away, too. Left me mighty high and dry."

Hagerman fell silent. Somewhere along the sheds in the yard chickens were clucking and far out on the range a gunshot flatted hollowly. The rancher stirred, glanced up.

"What I was getting at — I got a job here for you if you're willing."

"Riding shotgun over you?"

46

"More or less — but not for the reason you're maybe thinking. Hell, I ain't afraid of dying. Come close to it a couple of times already — and once you've been there, been near to dying, I mean, the next time don't scare you much. It's that I can't afford to let it happen."

"Afford?"

"Not money-wise. It's that there ain't nobody to take over Hash Knife was somebody to cut me down."

"You've got a son — and a daughter."

"Son!" Price Hagerman snorted. "Hell, you mean I've got a useless, unreliable, no-good boy — that's what I've got. And the girl — hell, females are for one thing only — marrying. She'll be marrying off one of these days, anyway, and moving on, so you have to count her out. . . . Aim to take care of her, sure — big dowry and all that, but it ain't having a son to take over the place, keep it going right."

"Ron looked all right to me," Starbuck said. "Maybe you don't give him a chance."

"I've given him plenty of chances. Messed up on every one. Flat-assed failed me. Hell, I don't dare turn nothing that's important over to him. Wouldn't be no need to hire on a foreman every now and then if he had anything good in him."

Starbuck said nothing, turned again to the window. The two riders had disappeared and now a small jag of cattle being herded by a solitary cowhand was moving toward the ranch from the hills.

47

"Which brings me to what I've got in mind," the rancher said. "Ain't never come right out and admitted it to anybody, but I am a bit jumpy about getting myself shot. Expect you can see why now."

"Then you figure there's something to the talk about a gunnie coming after you?"

"I reckon. I got a few enemies — more'n most, I guess. Man can't help making them when he sets out to build up something big as Hash Knife. And like I told you I plain can't afford to die right now. Have to stay in the saddle until Ron grows up and I'm able to trust him, or —" Hagerman paused, cocked his head to one side, peered at Shawn and added: "— or my girl finds herself a man who'd be strong enough and willing to take over."

The rancher let his words hang for a long breath while he continued to study Starbuck. Finally he straightened, and brought his hands together.

"So I'm offering you the job to stick around, keep me alive until the time comes when one or the other'll happen."

Shawn shook his head. "Obliged to you, but I'm not looking for work."

"Figured that, but I expect it costs money to go wandering around the country hunting for this Ben."

"Does. Have to stop every once in awhile, take a job to raise cash so's I can keep going."

"Then why not —"

"Just came off a job over New Mexico way. Fixed me up pretty good so there's no reason to hire out. If Ben's not here, I'll have to push on."

Price Hagerman sighed, brushed the sweat off his face. "Could make it worth your while — but I don't reckon that's any special inducement to you."

"No, sure isn't."

It was no unfamiliar problem to Starbuck. In his passage across the west he had several times encountered this situation where a father, doubting the abilities of his son, or sons, refused to relinquish the reins and step down. Sometimes there had been reason for the reluctance, but there were occasions when it was not justified.

"Don't mean to be sticking my nose into your family business," he said, "but could be you're figuring Ron short. Might pay to quit rawhiding him, give him another chance."

"Be a waste of time," Hagerman grumbled. "All he's wanting to do is lay around and go trotting off to town every time he can. Seems he can always find plenty to do there, what with whoring and drinking and gambling and such."

"Could be he's doing that because he feels there's nothing else for him — and forking manure's not much of a job for any man."

The rancher shifted. "Maybe it ain't but it keeps him out from under my boots, and there's nothing he can foul up while he's doing it."

Hagerman hesitated, glanced toward the outer

door as heels rapped on the bare wooden floor. A moment later Dave Archer stamped into the room. The foreman's face was taut, angry.

"Drawing my time," he said, halting in front of the rancher.

Price Hagerman's mouth tightened. "You quitting?"

"You're damn right I'm quitting! Took enough of your chewings — a whole blasted year of them, in fact! That's more'n enough for any man. You just get yourself another whipping boy."

"Easy enough done," Hagerman drawled. "But you ain't got no time coming. Wages due you won't near pay for them steers you let die."

"I let die!" Dave Archer shouted. "I ain't the only hired hand on this spread! Why the hell don't you try collecting from the rest —"

"Because you're the ramrod and the one responsible."

"Well . . . I ain't paying —"

"And you ain't drawing either. No, sir. What you've got coming will go against what you owe."

"I don't owe you a cent, Price," Archer said, his voice trembling with anger. "You know it."

"Owe me for twelve steers — over two hundred dollars. You got less'n a month's wages due. That won't cover but about half what they were worth."

The foreman's face had darkened to where it was almost purple as anger continued to mount within him. He brushed at his mouth, took a step forward. Hagerman's hand dropped casually upon Starbuck's pistol lying before him on the table. He looked up at Archer, eyes flat, features expressionless.

"When you ride out just be damned sure you don't let nothing of mine stick to your fingers — hear?"

Dave Archer's lips parted to make a reply, closed quickly as he thought better of it. Pivoting on a heel, he strode from the office.

Hagerman glanced at Shawn, a sly smile pulling at his mouth. "Foreman's job's open, seems. Sure you ain't interested?"

"I'm sure," Starbuck replied. "Give it to Ron."

"Only wish't I had the guts to," the rancher said, and, taking up Shawn's pistol by the barrel, handed it across the table.

Starbuck accepted the weapon, dropped it into its holster. Hagerman, rising, stepped to the door, looked into the yard.

"Dave always did have a short powder string. Expect he'll be back."

Shawn shook his head, moved up behind the rancher. He had seen pure hatred in Archer's eyes.

"Wouldn't hold my breath waiting for him, if I were you," he said. "It all right if I hang around a couple of days? Like to talk to your hired help about Ben."

"Do what you damn please," Price Hagerman said and turned back into his office.

51

7

Starbuck moved out into the bright, hot sunlight, paused briefly to get his bearings. It was also agreeable that he stay in the bunkhouse, he supposed, and crossing to the sorrel, he mounted and rode to the nearest of the three structures that housed the crew.

At that moment there was a quick rush of hooves. Dave Archer, a small carpetbag slung from the horn of his saddle, broke into the open beyond the long, low building, and, looking neither right nor left, pounded out of the yard. Shawn watched the man disappear behind the tamarisk windbreak while the thought occurred to him again that Price Hagerman was fooling himself if he thought the man would return and resume his job as foreman.

Halting in front of the bunkhouse, he dismounted and entered the rambling structure. It was considerably cooler and he paused just within the door, brushed sweat from his face and looked about. Two dozen or so bunks formed lines down either side as well as in the center of the rectangular room.

There was no one present, and, probing along the first row with his eyes, he located a bed that didn't appear to be taken. He'd park his gear there, he decided, and later, if someone claimed that particular bunk, he'd change to another.

Returning to the sorrel he obtained his saddle-bags and blanket roll, toted them into the building and dropped them on the chosen bed. He stood quiet then, thinking, considering the best course of action to follow in making inquiries.

Circle Hash Knife was a large spread with many riders — fifty, the rancher had said. There seemed little sense in simply going out on the range and seeking out each man singly. It would be much smarter to simply hang around the bunkhouses and talk to the punchers as they came in for meals or to sleep. In that manner he should be able to meet them all.

He could start that evening — not many hours away. The day crew would be riding in, being relieved by the men assigned to the nighthawk trick. Decided, he wheeled and once more entered the yard, intending to take the sorrel into the stable, give him a rub-down and a ration of feed. He hauled up sharp. Rhoda Hagerman, astride a fine looking tan and white mare, was waiting for him at the rack.

"You've moved in," she said, matter of factly.

"Be for a couple of days. Aim to talk to the crew."

Rhoda frowned, bit at her lower lip. She had changed clothing, now wore a blue silk shirt and a pair of close fitting black pants of lightweight material. Her boots were glove soft, artfully decorated with carefully stitched floral designs.

"Then you didn't sign on?"

"No. Be moving on soon as I've done my asking."

"Your asking?"

"About my brother, Ben. There's a chance some of your hired help knew him, or have maybe seen him. Fact is, he could be working for you right now. Your pa didn't know."

The girl nodded absently. "He wouldn't. Why don't you talk to Dave Archer? He's the one who'll —"

"He's gone — quit. Rode out a bit ago."

She stared at him. "Dave quit?"

Shawn pushed back his hat. "Can't say as I blame him much. Your pa's a little on the unreasonable side."

"You're not telling me something I don't already know. He offer you the job?"

"Had my choice — that one or one bodyguarding him."

"That's what I figured he'd talk to you about. He's more worried than he lets on."

"Worried, maybe, but he's not scared. He's afraid something will happen to him before your brother's able to step into his boots — or you find yourself a husband who can do it."

"He's going to be disappointed then if that's what he's waiting on. Not much chance of either coming true. You busy?"

"Not specially. Was figuring to look after my horse."

"That can wait. I'd like for you to take a ride

with me . . . to talk."

Shawn studied the girl in silence. It would take very little to become interested in her — and that was something he could not permit himself to do, not in her or any other woman. A life of his own would have to wait until he found Ben and had squared away all matters pertaining to Hiram Starbuck's estate.

"You bashful — or maybe afraid?" Rhoda asked, arching her brows. She had mistaken his reluctance and was finding it amusing.

He smiled, stepped up to his saddle. "Reckon there are a few things I'd be afraid of," he drawled, "but I don't think you're one of them."

Rhoda tilted her flat crowned Mexican hat to a more rakish angle and swung the mare around. "We'll go down by the creek. It's cool there."

They rode in silence from the yard, slanting southwest for a small grove of trees a mile or so in the distance. Arriving there they pulled up under a huge, spreading cottonwood. Shawn, dismounting, stepped to the mare's flank and extended his arms to help the girl down.

She gave him a pleased, quizzical look, allowed him to lift her easily from the saddle. Moving then to a log that lay half in, half out of the softly burbling creek, she found a seat, beckoned to him to do likewise.

Starbuck removed his hat, stepped to the stream and doused his face and head with the cool water. Drying with his bandana, he returned to her.

"I — I don't think I heard your first name," she said, fussing with her thick hair.

"Guess it wasn't mentioned. Happens to be Shawn."

She looked up, interested. "That sounds Indian. Are you part —"

"No, it's short for Shawnee. My mother once taught some children from that tribe. She liked the sound of the word, made it into a name for me."

"I see. . . . You haven't always lived in this part of the country, have you?"

"I was born in Ohio. Pretty well grew up there."

"I thought so. You talk better than most of the men around here. Pa sent me back to Virginia for awhile, trying to educate me. I hated it there."

"Home's always best," Starbuck murmured, looking off across the long flat glittering in the hot sunlight. Dust devils were whirling along the edge of the hills to the west.

"I was born on this place — right in the house where we live now. Ron, too. Pa came here when he was fifteen, back in 1830. Met my mother here, too. She was a San Antonio girl, came to visit some friends. She never went back."

"Took a lot of doing to build up a fine ranch like this. Plenty of money, too."

"There wasn't much money involved. Pa worked at all sorts of jobs until he got a chance to open a little store. You know the kind — general merchandise and such. He got to taking in cattle and horses for supplies, and then later on started trading for land.

"The war came along then. He wasn't for either side although he leaned to the South. Said they were fools, though, to think they could beat the North, with all its big cities and factories and the like. He figured it would be smarter to be a supply point for both, and that's what he did — sold cattle and horses to whoever had the money — hard money."

"And when it was all over he was a rich man with a big ranch."

"That's the way it worked out, all right," Rhoda said and then looked closely at Shawn. "Why? Is there something wrong with that?"

"No, guess not, only things didn't turn out so good for most people. War ruined them. There were plenty who lost everything they had."

"The war wasn't pa's fault. He just did what he thought best for himself and his family."

"Not everybody'll look at it that way. Some will figure he took advantage of the times, grabbed up all he could fast as he could."

Rhoda became silent. In the depths of the cottonwood's sprawling limbs a dove mourned softly. Somewhere along the creek a splash sounded as a raccoon or like small animal caught a fish for his meal.

"I suppose so," she said at length, "but isn't that how life is out here? The strong win out while the weak fall by the wayside."

"Same as it is everywhere, I suppose — not

that it makes it right. Once spent some time with a band of people who didn't believe in that. They lived together like a family, shared everything equal, the work as well as all the things they could make or grow. They didn't believe in greed or violence and if trouble hit them, they'd turn away from it, even pick up and move on if there wasn't another answer."

"A person would have little to show for a lifetime here on earth, feeling that way."

"Exactly the point. They believed in what the Bible says about not building any mansions. Could be they're right. You sure can't take any of it with you."

"Which is just what Pa would like to do," Rhoda said with a laugh. "If he can arrange it he'll take Hash Knife right up to heaven with him. . . . Or maybe it'll be down to the hot place."

"Means a lot to him, no doubt. That threat to kill him — there something to it?"

The girl frowned. "Of course."

"I mean, is there somebody in particular out to put a bullet in him? I know there's probably plenty who'd like to but never get farther than talking about it."

"He has a great many enemies."

"Only natural. Building this ranch up to what it is meant stepping on people, and he sure doesn't take much trouble trying to get along with folks. Saw a good sample of that today — Dave Archer."

"I know. My mother tried to change him when

she was alive but she didn't have much luck. He just rides iron-shod over everybody — friends or enemies. He's grown worse since Mama died — that changed him the wrong way."

"He's a mighty lonely man. Found that out from talking to him."

"I wondered about that. You were in there with him a good while. Expect he opened up with you more than anybody in a long time."

"He unwound himself plenty."

Rhoda sighed. "Expect it was good for him to open up, but it won't really make any difference. He'll always be the way he is. I guess only dying will end it."

"Too bad. Going to be hard on you and Ron if it happens. He'll be leaving behind a lot of hate that you'll have to face."

"I know — and it's more than just an if. Someone is coming to kill him — a man paid to do it."

Starbuck's head came up slowly. "You know that for certain?"

"I do."

"Who is he?"

"I don't know his name, only who it was that hired him."

Shawn didn't take his eyes off Rhoda's stilled, softly contoured face. "Who?"

"My brother — Ron."

8

For the space of several moments Starbuck said nothing. And then, "You want me to believe that?"

"Whether you do or not, it's the truth," Rhoda said in a lost voice.

Again he was silent. Finally, "You're saying that Ron wants his own pa murdered?"

She nodded woodenly.

"How do you know? He wouldn't have told you."

"I heard it from . . . well . . . a friend, a drummer that I got acquainted with one day when I was in town. While we were talking Ron passed by. Orly — that was my friend's name — didn't know he was my brother."

"Then how —"

"It came to him by accident. He overheard Ron talking to someone that was leaving on the stagecoach he'd just come in on. Ron was giving him the cash to hire a gunman. The person to be killed was Price Hagerman."

Frowning, Shawn studied the backs of his hands. Murder — killing was not uncommon, but for a son to deliberately plan the death of his father was something else again.

"You sure this Orly couldn't be mistaken?"

"I am. He recognized Ron the instant he saw

him, and he called Pa by name. Besides, there'd be no reason for him to make it up. He knew me only by Rhoda."

"When was this gunman to come?"

"No day was set. Ron told whoever it was that he was dealing with that he didn't want to know — that the killer was not to get in touch with him. He was to just ride in, get the job done, and ride on. That's why he paid for it in advance."

Starbuck got to his feet, began to pace slowly back and forth, eyes on the ground. Hired guns — paid-for assassinations — were no novelty to him, but the thought of an acquaintance, even one as recent as Ron Hagerman, arranging for the death of his father left him somewhat stunned.

"I take it that you haven't told your pa anything about it."

"No, of course not. Deep down Pa loves Ron — worships him, really. He's just hard on him because he wants him to be like himself. . . . I think he sees himself in Ron and wants to be certain he doesn't make the mistakes he did, and does all the things he should have done."

"Still, might be better to tell him."

"Why? It would break his heart — destroy him. Could you have told your father that this brother you're looking for — Ben — had hired someone to kill him?"

Starbuck paused, placed himself in Rhoda's position. "Reckon not," he admitted. All he could have done would be to watch close and hope to prevent it.

"I thought a lot about it, even considered going to Ira Blackburn about it, but I couldn't force myself to do that either. Family pride, I suppose. Anyway, what could he do? He's so old — and sort of useless."

"Picked me up quick enough. How did the word get out that a killer was coming after your pa?"

"I started it — with Ira. I wrote him a letter, had it mailed from San Angelo, warning him that it was about to happen. I signed it 'A Friend.' . . . I thought it might put Pa on his guard and maybe there was a chance Ira Blackburn would stumble onto the gunman when he showed up."

"It's got him watching close all right. Hadn't been in town thirty minutes when he jumped me. Then when I headed out this way, he followed. Expect he's a lot better lawman than most folks give him credit for being."

"I suppose. It's probably that no one has any respect for him. Pa browbeats him terribly — overpowers him like he does everybody else. You . . . you're the first man that I've ever seen stand up to him in my entire life. And to hit him like you did —"

Shawn shrugged. "You don't seem much afraid of him."

"I've never let myself show it but I guess he does sort of awe me. I've found the best way for me to get along with him is to act smart with him — be flip. He puts on a big show of being irritated by it but I think he's sort of pleased.

Anyway, I've got no problem with him."

Rhoda Hagerman just sort of lay back and floated with the current, taking everything for granted and accepting, come what may, Shawn realized. He wondered if it had occurred to her that all Hash Knife would be hers if Price Hagerman was told of Ron's scheme to have him killed. The rancher would immediately turn from son to daughter in such event.

Undoubtedly she had thought of it; Rhoda was a smart girl. But the idea apparently did not appeal to her. There was more heart and feeling within her than the facade of flippancy she exhibited to the outside world indicated.

And she was frightened. Starbuck detected that in her words and manner, in the urgency of her voice — and by the very fact that she had taken him, a stranger, aside and laid her troubles before him.

"What about Ron?" he said then, stating an obvious question: "Have you talked to him about it?"

"I thought about that. It was the first thing that came to my mind when Orly told me what he'd overheard. I planned to go straight to Ron, accuse him and have it out with him."

"But you decided against it?"

The girl nodded wearily. "It seemed best. Ron and I have never been close, like a brother and sister ought to be. I was afraid if I went to him that it would only widen the gap between us, force him to be even more distant than he is. Be-

63

sides — what could he do about it? He doesn't know who the killer is or when he'll come. . . . He couldn't stop it if he wanted to."

"Does he?"

"I'm not sure. Sometimes I think so, and then after a set-to like today's when Pa was especially nasty with him, I don't believe he does. I . . . I guess I've just followed the easiest course, let things rock along, hoping matters would work out — or that somebody would come along that I could talk to and maybe lean on for support. . . . Like you, Shawn."

Starbuck paused before the fallen tree. He sat down slowly. "No — don't depend on me."

Rhoda continued to study him, hope not fading from her eyes. "If it's money —"

"Not that. Expect to be here only a couple of days. It turns out this has been another wild goose chase, I'll have to ride on. Lost a lot of time this year already because I let myself get mixed up in other folks' troubles."

"It would probably be for only a month or so. Whoever it is coming for Pa is due. Been over a month now since it started."

"Ought to be others you could hire on."

"Who? There's nobody in Brasada, or here on the ranch. And the truth is, I'd be afraid to get just anybody. There are too many around who would just as soon someone would kill Pa. You're the only one I'd feel safe with and that I think could handle the job."

Abruptly Rhoda leaned forward, grasped

64

Starbuck's broad hands in her own. Overhead there was a quick whistling of wings as more doves came to rest in the cottonwood.

"Please, Shawn — help me! I'm afraid and I don't know which way to turn. Stay here for just a month — one month. If the killer hasn't shown up by then, you can ride out. . . . If not for my sake, for Ron's. He'll never be able to live with himself if it happens — I'm sure of that."

Starbuck stared off toward the hazy hills. It would mean thirty more days lost insofar as his search for Ben was concerned — assuming this trip to Hash Knife was for nothing. But should that be the topmost consideration in his mind? What was a month if, by his presence, he could save one man from death, prevent another from destroying himself? In the long run, perhaps, the days lost would mean little for him, but they could count for so much where Rhoda — where the entire Hagerman family, in fact — was concerned.

He got to his feet slowly, nodded. "All right," he said.

9

Rhoda was upright instantly. In the same motion she threw her arms about Starbuck's neck, and, going to tip-toes, kissed him firmly on the lips. He pulled back, surprised and frowning.

"Now, wait —"

"Thank you, Shawn — thank you from the bottom of my heart! For the first time in weeks I feel like I can draw a full breath."

His features were sober. "Don't bank too strong on me. Only so much I can do."

"I know. I'm not looking for miracles, but I'm sure if anyone can save Pa, it'll be you."

He made no reply, simply stood motionless looking down at her. She came only to his shoulder, he noticed, and despite the off-hand, devil take all impression she sought to convey, there was a strong need in her. That she was also a beautiful girl came to him again, and he hoped he'd not fail her confidence.

"Your pa," he said, that thought bringing Price Hagerman to the front of his mind again, "is going to wonder why I changed my mind about taking his offer. Have to come up with a pretty good reason. He's not an easy man to fool."

"I know that, and we'd better start by not going back to the house together. I know him —

he'd suspect I cooked up something with you."

Starbuck signified his agreement. "You head out now. I'll ride on for a spell, maybe talk to some of the help about my brother. Time I'm ready to turn around, I'll have a reason worked out."

Rhoda moved to where the mare waited, paused, allowed Shawn to take her arm, assist her onto the saddle. The small courtesies he paid her pleased her immensely, caused her eyes to glow. Smiling down at him, she lifted the reins.

"Thank you again, Shawn . . . I'll see you later at the house," she said, and spurred away.

He did not stir but remained where he stood, watching her as she rode off. Shawn Starbuck was not a man given to regrets once he had come to a decision, but he was wishing, nevertheless, the task of safeguarding Price Hagerman had not befallen his lot.

The circumstances were anything but comfortable. A son arranging for a faceless killer whose arrival was unknown to everyone — who could actually be on Hash Knife premises at that very moment masquerading as an employee!

Against such odds he was expected to perform the near impossible and fend off or ferret out the would-be assassin and prevent the death of Hagerman — Mr. Texas — a man all too many would like to see dead.

He grinned tightly, walked slowly to the sorrel, and, jerking the leathers free, went to the saddle. It would take a lot of doing on his part; it meant staying close to the rancher, enduring his slashing tongue, his brutal irony and utter disregard for others. He could expect to find little free time for himself.

He would need to watch Ron closely, too. Despite the agreement made with the killer, there could come a tip-off of some kind that the younger Hagerman would receive — and betray. If such did occur, Shawn realized, he must be aware of the fact and thus be in a position to move quickly.

Wheeling the gelding around, he followed the creek for a mile or two, hoping to encounter some of Hash Knife's riders. He saw none, and, vaguely disturbed now by a conscience that told him he should be near Price Hagerman if he was to carry out his promise to Rhoda, he cut back and returned to the ranch, coming into the yard from a different angle to the one he figured the girl had taken.

He rode straight to the stables, entered, and dismounting, set to stripping the sorrel of gear. That done, he stationed the big horse in a vacant stall, forked down a portion of hay, dumped a quart of grain into the manger and then retraced his steps to the yard.

Halting outside the wide door, he looked to the old hut where Hagerman maintained his office. It was dark inside the small structure but through the open entry he could see movement and reckoned the rancher was still there. . . . Best to get it said and done with, he decided, and immediately crossed over.

Price Hagerman, sitting at his table, looked around, a scowl on his browned face. Shawn spoke first, figuring it better to state the reason for his presence before being asked.

"I'm taking you up on that job offer."

The rancher's eyes narrowed. He leaned back in his chair, tugged at an end of his bushy mustache.

"Why?"

Starbuck had known that would be the man's first question. To him there had to be a reason behind everything, one that was always suspect.

"Just got to thinking about all that extra money. I can make good use of it."

It was a reason Price Hagerman could understand. He nodded, said, "Thought you had a plenty for awhile."

Starbuck's shoulders stirred. "Could use a new saddle — and I lost my rifle a time back. Extra cash'll pay for them. Anyway, all the time I was out I never ran into a single one of your hired hands. Big place. Talking to all of them is going to take longer than I figured."

The rancher continued to toy with his mustache for another few moments, then rocked forward. "All right. A hundred a month and found suit you?"

"Fine with me."

"Then move your belongings into the house. Be wanting you to do your eating and sleeping there. Got fourteen goddam rooms in the place and we're using about half."

"I can bunk with the crew," Starbuck said, protesting mildly. He would find it easier to come and go as well as make his inquiries from that point, he felt.

"Hell with that. Best you stick close if you're going to wet-nurse me."

Shawn grinned, having a quick vision of himself or anyone else being a nurse to Price Hagerman. "Whatever you say."

"Want you with me, no matter what. When I'm in here working, you're to be standing by. I go out on the range, you'll be siding me. Only time you'll be on your own is when I turn in for the night. That clear?"

"If that's how you want it. Going to need your help too in not taking any unnecessary chances."

"I don't aim to be ducking and dodging none. Got this ranch to run. Not about to start hiding out."

"I understand that, just asking that you don't take any needless risks."

"Depends on what you figure's needless. See about it later. Want you to get moved in. Tell the girl to fix you up in one of the extra bedrooms. If she ain't around, tell Salazar, she's the Mex woman we got to do the housekeeping and cooking . . . Be supper time pretty soon. I'll see you then."

Starbuck saw no signs of Rhoda when he lugged his saddlebags and blanket roll into the house and it was Salazar, a short, round-faced, smiling woman who conducted him to the second floor and led him into one of the chambers that opened off a long hallway.

Tossing his belongings onto a chair, he turned to the woman. *"Señorá —"*

"Mamacita," she corrected at once.

"Mamacita, where does the *patron* sleep? Which is his room?"

She gave him a puzzled frown and pointed to a door at the far end of the hall. "There. It is the room that was used also when the lady lived. There is a reason why you ask?"

Shawn nodded. "I've been hired to watch over the *patron.* I need to know where he will be at night."

Mrs. Salazar smiled approvingly. "I am pleased. There has been much worry for him."

Starbuck looked at her closely. "By who?"

"By the *muchacha.* Also by the boy, I think, but he talks but little. It is possible the *patron* himself worries but he is too proud of heart to let it be known."

"And by you?"

Mamacita smiled. "The *patron* I have known for more years than the children are old. I came here as a young woman. I have seen much, and I know much."

"You don't think he is in danger?"

"There is no doubt of such. There are many who hate him, but that has always been so — and is he not still alive? He spits in the face of those who would do him harm."

71

"This time it is different," Starbuck said quietly. "He'll not know the man who hopes to kill him. None of us will. If a stranger comes be sure to tell me. I shall be watching but I could be away and not see him."

"I will tell you, *señor.*" *Mamacita* Salazar paused. "How are you called?"

"Shawn."

She rolled the name over her tongue. It came out soft-edged and gentle. "A good name," she murmured and, turning, went back to the hall and down the stairs.

Starbuck waited until her footsteps had ceased and then entered the corridor. Walking quickly, he crossed to the door at its far end. Turning the knob, he stepped inside.

The room apparently was much the same as it had been when Eunice Hagerman was alive. Her mirror, combs and brushes were still laid out on the dresser. Pictures that evidently had meant much to her yet hung on the wall. Odds were, he guessed, her clothing still filled the drawers of the high chest and closet. Price Hagerman undoubtedly thought very deeply about his wife.

Feeling something of an unwelcome intruder, Shawn stepped to the two windows in adjacent walls. Both were open, and, looking out, he saw that it was a sheer drop to ground level and that there were no nearby trees or sheds that would permit entry from the yard. Anyone attempting to get at Hagerman would be compelled to use the inside stairway — unless there was an outside set of steps reaching the second floor at some point.

He descended to the lower floor, made a complete circle of the house. There was no means for gaining entrance except the doors of the main level. Relieved, he paused in the shade at the north end of the structure, brushed away the sweat gathered on his face. Guarding the rancher, once he was in his room, would likely be unnecessary. The killer would not risk coming into the house to seek out his target. . . . But just to be certain he'd suggest to Hagerman that he lock his door when he retired for the night.

Shawn glanced to the sun. It would be at least another hour before the evening meal would be served. He'd have time to clean up a bit — shave, put on a fresh shirt. Eating at a table as part of a family would be an experience he had been denied since Muskingum. That was a long time ago, it seemed.

10

Both Price and Ron were at the table when Starbuck came down to the well furnished dining room. The elder Hagerman greeted him with a curt nod.

"We take our meals on time around here," he said grumpily. "Supper's at six o'clock. Expect you to remember that."

Shawn made no answer, noting mentally that he'd not been advised of the specified hour, noticed also that Rhoda was not present. The rancher, at that moment, looked irritably toward the door that opened into the adjoining parlor and connecting foyer.

"Where the hell's that girl?" he muttered, and, rising, walked to the entrance and shouted: "Rhoda! What the devil's keeping you?"

Ron, features expressionless, shifted on his chair, seemingly careful to avoid Starbuck's glance. Price thumped back to his place at the head of the oblong carved Mexican table, settled himself testily. *Mamacita* appeared, coming through a different doorway carrying two large platters, one of fried steak, another piled high with fresh corn and boiled potatoes.

"Get it all in here, Salazar," the rancher ordered. "We ain't waiting no longer. She knows what time we eat."

"*Si, patron,*" the woman replied, and, placing the food before him, turned back to her kitchen.

Hagerman helped himself to the meat and vegetables, passed them on to Ron. A rustle at the parlor door drew their attention, and, looking around, Shawn saw Rhoda. He rose to his feet, caught up instantly by the beauty of her.

She had pulled back her dark hair, secured it with a ribbon that matched the pale blue satin dress she was wearing. Ron paid her scant attention but Price Hagerman, a forkful of meat halfway to his mouth, hesitated, stared.

"You going to a ball or something?"

The dress, tight fitting about the waist, was cut low to reveal her ample bosom. Its full, flowing skirt brushed the floor. A small pink cameo hung from a fine gold chain at her throat, contrasted against the sun-tinted duskiness of her smooth skin.

She nodded to all, smiled at Shawn as he drew back her chair and seated her. Then her eyes, half challenging, met those of her father.

"No. I just felt like dressing up a bit, that's all."

"You ain't never done it before."

"Oh, I think I have. You probably didn't notice. Be a good thing if we'd all do it more often."

Hagerman grunted his disapproval at the thought of a man dandying himself just to sit down and eat a meal at his own table, and resumed his food. Ron, sullen and silent, took no part in the conversation.

Mamacita Salazar entered again, bringing more fare and smiling broadly when she beheld the girl who was obviously her personal pride and delight.

"Did you find out anything about your brother?" Rhoda asked when the supper was fully underway.

Shawn said, "Not yet. Haven't had a chance to do much talking."

"After the crew's through eating will be a good time," she suggested. "The men usually hang around the bunkhouse playing cards and the like."

A silence fell over the room after that, broken finally by Price Hagerman. Without looking at Ron, he said, "You get that manure moved?"

The younger man nodded woodenly, said, "Yes."

"Tomorrow I want you to ride down to the line shack on Bull Creek, see that it's got plenty of grub stored up. Aim to have a crew working there next week and there ain't no sense of them wasting time riding back and forth to eat. You figure you can do that?"

"I can, Pa," Ron replied in a weary sounding voice.

"You know what kind of grub there ought to be there — stuff that won't spoil and don't take much fixing?"

"I know —"

"All right, see to it, now. I'll be riding over

next day to see if you done it."

"Be no need for that."

"Yeh, reckon there will be," Hagerman said mildly, and shifted his attention to Starbuck. "You get moved in?"

Shawn said, "I'm all set. Fine quarters — may have trouble sleeping."

"Oh, you'll get used to it," Rhoda said quickly as if fearing he might make a change.

"Sure you will," the rancher added, again pausing, gaze on his daughter. He swung his eyes to Shawn and a thoughtfulness came into them. He smiled faintly as if pleased by what had occurred to him. "Ain't no sense at all you staying with the crew — not when we got plenty of room here."

"How long will you be around?" Ron asked, a note of surprise in his voice as he spoke to Starbuck for the first time.

"Hard to say."

"Pa hired him on as . . . well . . . a bodyguard," Rhoda volunteered. "Guess we forgot to tell you."

Ron nodded glumly. "Yes, you did. Last I heard he was going to be here just long enough to see about this brother he's hunting."

The girl considered her brother narrowly. "Don't you like the idea of him being Pa's bodyguard?"

The younger Hagerman's shoulders stirred. "It ever make any difference what I like?" he asked, and, rising abruptly, wheeled from the table and left the room.

Price watched his departure with no particular interest. "Guess you had yourself a look at my place this afternoon — seen you riding out with my daughter," he said, coming back to Starbuck. "Like what you saw?"

There was a different note in the rancher's voice as he made the comment and asked his question, one that indicated his approval of the incident.

"Sure did," Shawn said. "Take a few days for a man to see it all."

"We'll do that together," Hagerman said, bobbing his head decisively. "Finest piece of land in this part of Texas. Got two hundred thousand acres and there's damned little of it that ain't usable. . . . Plenty of water — reaches all parts.

"Some other things I'd like to show you, too. There's a flat to the south of here where a man could grow hay and grain, cut down on his feeding costs . . . Once in a spell we have a dry summer and the range don't turn out so good. Be smart to do some feeding when that happens, keep the stock in good shape."

"You're lucky down here," Starbuck said. "Been on a few ranches where they have to do that regularly."

"Know that. Mighty hard to beat this country. Well, expect I'd best be turning in, leave you two alone. Young folks like you got more to talk about than an old stud like me."

"Favor I want to ask of you," Starbuck said, delaying the rancher with a lift of his hand. "Went over this house today. I figure it'll be a good idea if you'd lock your door when you go to bed."

Hagerman's eyes brightened. "Lock my door inside my own house! I'll be goddamned if I will!" he shouted, once more the man Shawn knew him to be.

"Now, Pa," Rhoda broke in. "You hired Shawn to do a job. Ought to let him do it."

Price got to his feet. He appeared much older than at first look, Starbuck thought. His big frame seemed to sag a bit and his eyes were tired in their deep hollows. It was at the end of day that age usually showed its haggard face.

"All right, whatever you say. . . . One hell of a note, howsomever, when a man has to bolt the door to his own bedroom," he declared, and, pivoting, left the room.

Rhoda stood before the full length mirror in her room and studied herself critically. She had hoped to spend the remainder of the evening with Shawn, but shortly after her father had retired he had excused himself politely and taken his leave. Not much later she had watched him, wide shouldered and erect on his big sorrel, ride from the yard. He was probably headed for town — but whether it was to keep an eye on Ron or to pass some time in one of the saloons she could only guess.

But the trouble she had gone to fixing up herself had not been wasted. Shawn had been impressed — and Pa! He was already teaming them up in his mind! He was transparent as glass — all that talk about the ranch, that showing it to him personally and pointing out its advantages and possibilities.

Rhoda smiled, moved to the cushioned chair by the window and sat down. She had news for Pa. She was far ahead of him. The moment when she first saw Shawn Starbuck she had recognized that he was a man to quicken the pulse of any woman; and then when he had smacked Pa on the jaw she decided he was the man she wanted — and would have, come fire or brimstone.

He was vastly different from the other men she'd known — so serious, so intent and so determined in the manner he went about things. Like this brother he had not seen for so many years and was seeking. He had made it clear that it was a mission he would see through to its end.

She would have to change his mind on that score. There would be no need for him to continue his wandering about over the country searching for Ben in order to settle his father's estate. She had heard most of the story — after Pa had ordered her out of the office so they could talk. The window had been open and it had been simple to just stand there and listen.

Once Shawn became her husband he would forget all about the inheritance, probably small, that awaited him. He'd have all the fortune he'd

80

ever want, being half owner of Hash Knife which she was certain Pa would make her — and Shawn. In fact, the way he felt about Ron at the moment, she could end up getting it all.

Rhoda considered that thought. Up to Shawn's riding into the scene, she'd never given the matter of being part owner of the ranch any deliberation. She had simply sat back, lived the life that was handed her without question, taking all things for granted. But Shawn Starbuck's coming put a different light on it; she guessed she should now take more interest in Hash Knife and become a bit more aggressive where it was concerned.

That she was more like Pa had long ago become clear to her, while Ron was said to take after their mother — and that made it easier. Ron had already done a pretty fair job of cutting the ground out from under himself; it would take little effort — even if Pa never learned that he had been the one to make a deal with the killer — for him to finish it.

But Shawn would require careful handling. He was no ordinary man ready to jump at the chance of getting himself a wife, a fine ranch and a fortune all in the same ball of wax. She would have to make it doubly attractive to him — and the answer to that lay in herself. *Me,* she thought, rising and beginning to undress. *I'll have to be the key.*

Shawn Starbuck was one in whom honor ran strong and deep; it was a major factor in gov-

81

erning his life — thus it at once became his most vulnerable point. Perhaps such scheming was cold-blooded, even ruthless, but Rhoda could see nothing wrong with it.

In this world when you finally came to know what you wanted above all else, you simply set out to get it. That had been the way Pa had made Hash Knife into what it was, the self-same system he had used to become the biggest and most powerful — and richest — rancher in southwest Texas. She could see no reason why she shouldn't follow his example.

Laying the blue satin dress aside, she removed the remainder of her underclothing and crossed to the dark wood dresser standing against the wall. Opening a bottom drawer, she rummaged about and located the nightgown she had purchased one time while visiting in the East. Pulling it over her head, she smoothed it against her. It was a light shade of pink, outrageously thin, and clung closely to her.

Turning, she surveyed herself in the mirror critically, and then, satisfied, nodded. It should do the trick and break down any man — even one so apparently straight-laced as Shawn Starbuck. . . . And there was no time like the present to get started at the task. Moving on to the chair near the window, she sat down to await his return.

11

Starbuck was not sure in his own mind what he expected to learn or accomplish by trailing the younger Hagerman into Brasada. It had simply occurred to him, as he sat at the table with Rhoda and Price, listening to the hoof beats of Ron's departing horse, that it was what he should do.

The rancher had said his son frittered away his time on gambling, liquor and women; if true, he would be associating with the hard-case lot among whom a hired killer, being a stranger in town, could expect to find friends. Therefore, observing them, listening, if possible, to their conversations, could result in a clue that would lead to the identity of the killer.

It had been somewhat difficult to leave. It was clear that Rhoda wanted to talk, to spend time in the parlor or perhaps out on the gallery where several big leather chairs had been placed and it was a great deal cooler. But the urge to keep an eye on Ron pushed at him steadily and he had ridden out.

The remembrance of Rhoda, the utter beauty of her, however, hung in his mind like a misty wraith, and it was not until he turned into the settlement's main street that the vision dissolved.

There were only a few persons abroad he

noted as he angled the sorrel toward the hitchrack at the side of The Chinaberry. Brasada was a small town, existed mostly for the convenience of Hash Knife and the three or four other ranches in the area, thus the list of permanent residents was short.

Halting at the rack, Starbuck dismounted, tied the gelding securely and stepped up onto the porch of the saloon. He would as soon Ron did not see him; that was sure to convince the younger Hagerman that he was being spied upon — which was, of course, partly true — and believing such Ron would likely avoid his usual haunts and companions.

Stopping just outside the saloon door, Shawn glanced inside. He saw Dave Archer immediately. Hash Knife's one-time foreman was sitting at a table with two other riders, morosely nursing a drink and evidently brooding over the injustice of Price Hagerman's actions.

The rancher had been unduly harsh, Starbuck thought, but it was none of his business.

Ron was not in The Chinaberry, he saw after touring the room with a probing glance. He could be upstairs in one of the rooms that lay off the balcony, and Shawn gave thought briefly to making inquiry of Nate or of Artha, if she was available, as to the probability, and then put it aside. He'd check the other saloons in town first.

Accordingly, he turned back to the street. A short distance farther along was THE KAFFI-KORN, which appeared small and seemed to have little light. Across the way and beyond several doors was a somewhat better illuminated barroom that bore the sign, THE PACK SADDLE. As far as he could tell there were no other saloons in Brasada; locating Ron should not be difficult.

The Kaffikorn had two customers lounging against a short, crudely constructed bar in the rear of its dimly lit interior; neither of them was Hagerman. Shawn crossed over to The Pack Saddle. It was enjoying slightly better patronage. Half a dozen men were hanging around the counter watching a seventh engaged, without music, in a stomp dance with a worn looking woman in soiled yellow. The puncher was physically enthusiastic but the expression on the woman's rouge-marked sallow face was one of utter exhaustion.

Ron Hagerman was not the energetic dancer and he was not among the six at the bar. Puzzled, Starbuck moved away from the door and paused in the shadows to consider. Could there be another town close by where Ron had gone?

He decided such was unlikely. No mention had been made of any settlement other than San Angelo and it was much too far distant. It had to be Brasada. His thoughts swung back to The Chinaberry, the second floor rooms where Artha and the women like her plied their trade. That's where he'd find Ron. . . .

All speculation came to a halt as the familiar figure of Hagerman, in company with a young girl, emerged from the doorway of a two-storied house a few strides away. The barely legible sign overhanging the walk designated it as MA CONVERCE'S ROOMING HOUSE. Ron and the girl hesitated momentarily and then moved toward Shawn slowly, evidently pointing for the small wooded square at the end of the street.

Trapped, Starbuck drew back into the deep shadows of the passageway alongside The Pack Saddle, unable to do anything other than remain hidden in the darkness. Almost at once Hagerman's voice came to him.

"Nothing's changed, Stell." His voice was low, discouraged. "Only wish I could say it had."

"But you said it would be soon! I'm so tired of waiting — holding on."

"Maybe you think I'm not!" There was impatience in Hagerman's tones now. "I told you it would take time. Told you that right at the start."

"I know, but it's going on longer than I figured. And Ma keeps ragging at me about it — always wanting to know when we're getting married. . . . I think she knows, Ron."

"Knows what?"

"Well . . . that we . . . that when we go off to the park at night, we —"

"What of it? Said we'd get married, didn't I? And we will."

"But when? That's what Ma and me keep wondering."

"Soon as we can."

"Couldn't we just forget everything here, move on to somewheres else? You could get a job on some ranch and —"

Ron swore deeply, halted, turned his face to the girl. They were almost directly in front of The Pack Saddle and weak light filtering through one of its dust smudged windows fell upon the pair. Stell was very young, Starbuck noted, no more than fifteen, perhaps sixteen at most.

"You think I'm giving up my claim on Pa's place? Just walking off, leaving it? Not by a jugful! I've earned my share of Hash Knife — earned it the hard way." He paused, added in more even tones, "No, I'm not throwing it all away."

"But for me you said once that you'd —"

"What's wrong with you, Stell? Don't you want to be rich? Don't you want to have servants and pretty clothes and a carriage and all the fine things that'll make you a lady?"

"Sure — of course I do," the girl replied, moving on. "But I just can't wait forever, Ron. . . . Sometimes I think I'd be better off tying up with some regular fellow, one who maybe ain't going to get all the things you say you'll have when your pa dies."

"You been talking to some other man?" Hagerman's voice was suddenly sharp.

"Well, not exactly. Always plenty of them coming to the house, renting rooms and such, and trying to spark me —"

"By God, Stell — you'd better not —"

"Never said I did, only that I sometimes get to wondering if —"

The girl's plaintive tones faded out of range. Starbuck, feeling somewhat embarrassed, sighed in relief. They hadn't noticed him.

He stared after them thoughtfully. What he had heard verified much of the story Rhoda had told him. Although Ron had not come right out and mentioned the fact that he expected the death of Price Hagerman shortly, he had indicated their future together began with that moment, which he had given her to understand would be soon.

Ron was having it rough. Price Hagerman dominated his life completely, so much so that he was less than a stable hand in stature on his father's own ranch and was also being forced to meet secretly in the dark with the girl he planned to marry — a girl who was, incidentally, growing impatient.

Ron's response to her urging had betrayed a strong note of anxiety — and that could mean trouble. The younger Hagerman, already pushed to the edge by Price, could become desperate if he believed he was to lose Stell.

It simply worsened a bad situation, and Shawn realized he would have to keep an even closer watch over the rancher. Ron could go over the edge, not wait for the man he had hired but take matters into his own hands. Starbuck had learned long ago how unpredictable a man turned quietly hopeless could become; even the meekest often turned, transformed into a tower of violence.

Moving back to the edge of the walk, Shawn glanced toward the square. Ron and Stell were vague outlines melting into the dark shadows beneath the trees. Maybe he should try to do something about the situation existing between the rancher and his son, see if he somehow couldn't promote a little better understanding between the two.

That would solve many of the problems that faced the family, although it would have no effect on the impending arrival of the gunman Ron had hired. . . . If he actually had done so . . .

Starbuck frowned as that came suddenly into his mind. He had no proof that a murder had been arranged; he had only Rhoda's word — word that had been based on information given her by a chance acquaintance. Could the whole thing be a lie? If so — whose lie? And why?

The person supposedly telling Rhoda of the arrangement — Orly or some such name — would have nothing to gain as far as he could see; by simple logic then it would be a lie on Rhoda's part — one designed to further discredit her brother and enhance her own interests. But would Hash Knife mean that much to her? She had given him the impression of caring little for the ranch — was that all a show, an out and out act for his benefit?

Starbuck swore suddenly, violently. Why the

hell had he let himself get mixed up in such a mess — a family mess at that? He must have been out of his head when he let himself get talked into becoming a part of the Hagerman quarrel!

Disgusted with himself and all things in general, Shawn stepped out into the street, slanted for the brightly lighted Chinaberry. He'd have himself a drink, cool off a bit and then return to the ranch. . . . If he hadn't already given his word to both Rhoda and Price Hagerman he'd pack up and move on.

There was one thing he could do, however; he would jump Ron about hiring a killer, demand to know if he actually had done such a thing. If he could get a straight answer to that question then he would at least know more about whom he could trust on Hash Knife.

12

The Chinaberry's clientele had increased some-what, Starbuck noticed when he crossed the saloon's porch and entered. Someone was at the piano playing in an uncertain, lonely fashion, ignored by most of the crowd gathered now about a man in checked suit and derby who was performing card tricks at one of the tables.

Dave Archer and the same group who had been with him earlier were now slouched against the bar, and as Shawn made his way up to the counter, Hash Knife's ex-foreman paused in whatever he was saying and eyed the tall rider coldly.

"Good seeing you again," Nate greeted, nodding and smiling. "Have any luck finding that brother of yours?"

"Not yet," Starbuck replied and ordered himself a drink. "Looks like you're doing pretty well."

"About usual for this time of week," the barman said. "Saturdays and Sundays — them's our big nights."

Shawn took up the shot glass Nate placed before him, had a swallow of the liquor. Artha detached herself from the card-sharp's admirers, swaggered toward him.

"Well, if it ain't my drifter friend!" she said

breezily. "Figured when I seen you next it'd be in the calaboose."

"Came close to going there," Starbuck grinned and, at the woman's questioning glance at his drink, motioned for Nate to pour her a portion also.

Artha downed the rye, cocked her head to one side and studied Shawn. "You're a kind of puzzlement to me. You buy me drinks then don't make a try at collecting."

Nate laughed. "When you say that you're admitting he's the first gentleman you ever met —"

"Gentleman!" Dave Archer spat out the word as if it were hot. "He's a dirty, job-stealing bastard, that's what he is!"

Shawn wheeled slowly to face the man a few steps farther down the bar. Nate spoke up anxiously.

"Now, Dave, don't go kicking up a ruckus —"

"The hell with you!" Archer snarled and hurled the glass he was holding at the saloonman. "Keep out of this!"

Nate caught the tumbler against his chest, swore into the abrupt stillness that fell across the room. Shawn tensed as he saw Archer's palm riding the butt of the pistol on his hip. He flicked Artha with a glance.

"Best you move out of the way."

Immediately the woman backed off. A man standing beside Archer caught at his shoulder. "Come on, Dave, let's take a walk down to The Saddle — see what's going on."

Archer shook him off angrily, began to ease forward. Starbuck pulled a full step away from the bar.

"Either take your hand off that gun — or use it," he said in a low voice.

Dave Archer halted, head slung forward on his bull-neck, eyes burning. Someone in the room upset a bottle. The crash of its fall was loud in the warm hush. Archer's stare locked with that of Starbuck's, held, dropped. A hard grin pulled at his mouth.

"Reckon I don't need iron to learn you a lesson at that," he said, sliding a glance at his friends now lined up somewhat apart from him and watching silently.

Shawn folded his arms across his chest. "Best thing you can do is go on about your business. We've got no quarrel."

"The hell we ain't! Was you that rooked me out of my job!"

Starbuck's eyes flared slightly with surprise. He shook his head. "Had nothing to do with it."

Archer jerked off his hat, slapped it down onto the counter. "You saying you're not working for Hagerman?"

"No, happens I am, but —"

"Then you're lying! I'm out a good job and you're working for him. Not hard to add that up."

"You quit. Was all your own doing."

"Sure . . . sure, but ain't it mighty goddam funny that on the day Price called me in on the

93

carpet for a chewing, you show up."

"Was just the way it worked out."

"The hell! You saying Hagerman never sent for you? That knowing you'd show up today he called me in, raised so much cain and such that he knew I'd quit so's he could hire you on?"

Starbuck shrugged. "From what I've seen of Price Hagerman he'd not go to that much bother if he wanted to fire you. He'd plain tell you straight out you were through. . . . Nothing at all to what you're bitching about."

"You're a goddam liar!" Archer shouted, and lunged.

Shawn took a hasty back step, caught a spur. He rocked against the bar, saved himself from going down by flinging an arm across its top, sagged as Archer's fist smashed into his unprotected belly.

Dave's friends yelled their delight, spread out to form a circle. Archer, grinning broadly, nodded confidently at them and swung again.

Starbuck, hanging against the counter, came to life suddenly. He threw up his left arm, neatly blocked the blow, sent a stinging right to Archer's head. The foreman staggered back, surprise and pain blanking his features.

Shawn moved quickly into the center of the ring, getting clear of the counter. Hands at his sides he considered Dave Archer.

"No need for this —"

"The hell there ain't," the dark faced man ground out savagely and rushed forward again, hands swinging wildly.

Starbuck dropped instinctively into the stance old Hiram had taught him — elbows crooked, fists knotted and ready, one foot ahead of the other. As Dave drove in, he jabbed the man sharply with a left, smashed him hard on the nose with a right and danced lightly away.

Shouts went up in the saloon. A voice said: "He's one of them fancy boxers!"

"Look at that belt he's wearing. . . . Must be a champion or something."

From his place behind the bar Nate shook his head. "Expect it would've been smarter for Dave if he'd used that gun of his'n."

Archer, furious, heard none of it. He recovered his balance, pivoted, came surging in again. Shawn took a glancing blow on the shoulder, traded it for a straight shot at the man's jaw. His balled fist missed as Archer slipped on something spilled on the floor. Before he could fade back, Dave's arms were about his middle, locked tight.

Palms open, Starbuck clapped them sharply to the man's ears. Archer howled, released his grip and staggered away. Shawn, temper within him rising, was upon him before he could recover. Driving a quick left into the belly, he followed with a right to the jaw, another left to Archer's mouth that brought blood.

Scarcely breathing hard, he pulled off, moving lightly on his feet. The saloon was once more in silence as Dave came about, shuffling uncertainly. He seemed at a loss as to where he was or what he was doing. Abruptly he regained his bearings, halted, glared at Shawn.

Blood smeared his chin and lips. One eye was closing rapidly. He shook his head to clear it, swore deeply. Starbuck faced him from across the circle.

"I'm willing to call it quits if you are."

"No, by God!" Archer rasped through his heavy breathing and moved in again, this time more cautiously.

Shawn easily sidestepped the advance, flicked Dave across the eyes with a stinging left, smashed him on the ear with a right that cracked loud when it landed. He was tiring of the senseless fight, was hoping to end it quickly now.

Archer reeled to one side, spun awkwardly, swung a wild, looping right. It caught Shawn going away, barely grazed him. Off balance, Dave stumbled forward. Starbuck seized the man by the shoulders, whirled him about, shoved him roughly into the arms of his friends.

"Here — look after him."

Deliberately turning his back, Starbuck moved to the bar, nodded at the bottle Nate still held in his hand. Behind him Dave Archer, supported by a man on either side, stared after him with glazed eyes while a dull hate tore at his features.

"Damn you — I ain't done yet! Not yet!"

Shawn took the glass of liquor the barman had poured, sipped it, shook his head. "You are for now. Maybe another time."

"There'll be another time — that's for goddam sure!" Archer yelled. "Bet on it."

"I'll do that," Starbuck said indifferently, and lifted his glass again.

Archer jerked free of the men at his shoulders, snatched up his hat. Pulling it on, he wheeled, headed for the door. Shawn came fully about to face Nate as a scattering of congratulations came from the crowd. Resting his elbows on the counter, he sighed.

"Glad that's over with."

He felt someone at his side, looked around. Artha said, "You want to come up to my room, I'll doctor your hurts."

Nate laughed loudly. "What hurts? Dave never touched him — hardly." He wagged his head admiringly. "You sure are something with them fists of yours!"

Starbuck reached into his pocket for a coin to pay for his drinks. The saloonman pushed his hand away.

"No, sir! It's on the house. Show was worth it."

A chorus of agreement went up from the onlookers standing near. Shawn nodded, said, "Obliged. . . . Now I reckon I'd best be getting back."

"To Hagerman's? You working for him like Dave claims?"

"I am — but not as his foreman. That job's still open, I expect." He looked down at Artha.

97

"Appreciate your offer, but I'm fine."

She gave him a slow smile. "Anytime — hurt or not, I'll be waiting."

"Be remembering that," he replied and started to pull away.

Nate reached out, stayed him. Leaning forward he said, "Probably be smart was you to keep off the road going back to Hagerman's."

Shawn frowned. "That so?"

The saloonman bobbed his head. "Dave's been kind of the kingpin around here, him being foreman of Hash Knife and such. You taking him down like you did ain't going to set good with him. I sure wouldn't make myself no easy target."

"Thanks, I'll keep it in mind," Starbuck murmured, and moved on for the door.

13

The night was cool, the street deserted when Starbuck stepped into the open. He took a long stride to his right, removed himself from the silhouetting doorway and pulled up close against the front of The Chinaberry, and waited.

There was doubt in his mind that Dave Archer would go so far as to ambush him; it would be a witless move on the part of Hash Knife's dismissed foreman since there actually was no ground for trouble between them. But he hardly knew Archer while Nate was well acquainted with the man, thus he felt it wise to heed the warning.

He stalled out two or three quiet minutes and when nothing happened crossed the remaining length of the porch. Activity within The Chinaberry had resumed — the plinking of the piano, the muted hub-bub of conversation punctuated now and then by a laugh — all signifying that his encounter with Dave Archer was already on the way to being forgotten.

In the saddle he paused to throw his glance down the street toward the park where he had last seen Ron Hagerman. There was no sign of him and the girl, and he reckoned they were still somewhere among the deep shadows of the trees.

He gave some thought to the possibility that Archer could take out some of his vengeance on Ron, a Hagerman, and considered briefly seeking him out, warning him or perhaps even suggesting they ride back to the ranch together. After a moment he brushed the idea aside; Archer would not likely harm Ron — they had a common enemy in Price Hagerman.

Touching the sorrel with his rowels, Shawn cut around behind the buildings lining the street and followed out the narrow alley laying there until he reached the end of the settlement. Coming to that point amid the frantic barkings of several dogs, he then veered southwest until he came to a low run of sandhills that paralleled the road to Hash Knife and remained on that course until he had arrived at the ranch.

The house was in total darkness, he saw as he rode along the edge of the yard to the barn. A lamp glowed weakly in the windows of the center bunkhouse, left on for later comers, he supposed, or perhaps it was being used by one of the more studious hands reading a book or a magazine. Stabling the gelding, he paused at the water trough, washed his face and neck of the sweat crusted on his skin from the encounter with Archer, and then quietly made his way to his room.

He didn't bother to light up, simply stripped down to his drawers and crawled into the bed. He was tired. It had been a long day, and despite Nate's claim, there were a few sore places along his ribs where Dave Archer's fists had smashed hard — or it could have been the effects of the bear-hug the man had sought to apply.

Throwing his arms wide, spreading his legs, he stretched, enjoying the feel of cool sheets, the softness of the mattress and yielding springs. It had been a good many years since he'd known such luxury, such comfort.

The door latch clicked softly. Instantly, Starbuck froze. He swore silently, recalling that his gunbelt hung on the bedpost an arm's length away. To get it he would have to rise, lunge forward. Tense, he waited.

A breath of perfume came to him. A faint rustling sounded and a vague shadow moved toward the bed. The springs squeaked quietly.

"I thought you'd never get back," Rhoda's voice said in mild protest.

Starbuck came out of the bed in a single bound. Snatching up his pants, he drew them on and crossed to the table. Lifting the chimney of the lamp standing upon it, he struck a match to the wick, replaced the glass cylinder and turned.

Rhoda, dressed only in a light gown, was smiling up at him. She had removed the robe she'd been wearing and dropped it into a chair. Hugging her knees, she shook her head.

"It would be smart to turn down that lamp, keep it dark in here."

"Smart thing is for you to get out," Shawn replied.

"Best we be quiet, too," she continued, ignoring his words. "Pa still thinks of me as his unwed daughter whose honor needs defending. He hears us, you can expect to be looking at the muzzle of his shotgun."

"Not a chance. You're leaving — now."

Rhoda made a small face, began to adjust her hair, smoothing out the thick folds that spread about her shoulders.

"You were gone a long time. Did you find out what you wanted to know about Ron?"

He shook his head. "About all I learned was he has a girl — one named Stell."

"Oh, her —"

"Seems they'd like to get married only they can't because of your pa. It true he won't permit it or is Ron just telling her that to stall things off?"

"It's true, all right. Pa won't listen to it. Says Stell Converce is plain trash and if Ron can't find quality to marry, he'll have to stay single."

One more reason for hate, Shawn thought.

"If I was Ron I'd tell Pa to go to hell. Stell's not much, but then who is in this country? In the beginning everybody had to scratch for a start."

Starbuck leaned back against the wall. "Don't think she's much interested in what Ron will get. Sounded more like she was in love with him."

"I suppose she is. That mother of hers is in love, too — with the money Ron'll have. Won't hurt them to wait. Stell's only sixteen. . . . Are you coming back to bed or do I have to come after you?"

"Neither one. You're getting out of here — fast. I'm not about to get all mixed up in something I might not be able to stop."

"Why stop anything? Pa'd give his right arm to have you in the family. Wants you . . . well . . . much as I do."

"Don't fool yourself, Rhoda. I'm not for you, not for any woman, in fact."

"Why?"

"Ben — I'm not settling down until I find him. After that I can think about a wife and a home of my own."

Rhoda's shoulders stirred indifferently. "Forget about your brother. This estate you're trying to settle won't be but a drop in a rain barrel to what you'd get out of Hash Knife — and I'd come with it."

"Mighty tempting, all right, only I couldn't take it, or you, on that basis."

"Why not?"

"If you don't know then it would be a little hard for me to explain," he said, and hoping to change the subject, added: "I've been thinking about Ron. There a chance you could be wrong about him — about him hiring a killer, I mean?"

Rhoda's lips drew into a petulant line. "No, there's not."

"Was wondering if that friend of yours — Orly, I think you called him — maybe didn't get it straight. He could have been mistaken in it being Ron."

"There was no mistake — and he wouldn't lie

about it. What would he have to gain?"

"I don't know. Just hard to believe your brother would pull a stunt like that."

"You don't know him. You're judging him by yourself and this Ben you're looking for. Not all families are like yours, close and loving. In some it's a matter of everyone looking out for himself and the devil take the hindmost."

"That the way you figure it ought to be?"

"Is it so wrong? I know what I want and how to get it. It was the same with Pa — still is. What he wants he goes after . . . and gets. I take it from him, I guess."

"Which leaves Ron for the devil."

Rhoda shrugged, her soft white shoulders moving gracefully under their thin covering.

"Like somebody once said, that's life."

Shawn eyed her critically. "You've changed your thinking some."

"How?"

"What happened to Hash Knife didn't seem to interest you much before. Now you sound like you're out to take it all."

"That so strange? Happens I never had a reason to care about it before. . . . now I have."

He gave her a hard smile. "If that reason's me, best forget it."

"You mean you'd not be interested in someday owning a place like this?"

"Sure. Be lying to you if I said I wouldn't. Have to be under different circumstances, however."

"What circumstances?"

"That what I got I came by it honestly, not by cheating somebody else."

"Suits me," Rhoda said airily. "Ron will get his share and I'll take mine — a half interest. If I tell Pa what the deal is between us, he'll jump at the chance to change his thinking. That way you'll be coming by your share honestly. That ease your conscience?"

"It might, if I was interested — which I'm not."

"Oh, I think you would be if you'd take a little time to consider."

"No need. I know how I feel."

"You only think you do. Go ahead, do some studying on it tomorrow . . . and the next day. Right now, are you going to stand there against the wall the rest of the night, or are you turning down that lamp and getting back in this bed?"

Starbuck folded his arms, stared at her silently. She fluffed her hair, smiled.

"You act like you've never known a woman before."

Face expressionless, Shawn pulled away from the wall, reached for the lamp. He paused as the quiet thud of hooves rose faintly from the yard below.

Turning, he crossed quickly to the window in three long strides. Keeping back from the frame he looked down. A rider was moving slowly along the edge of the hard pack, pointing for the deep shadows beyond the near bunkhouse.

Wheeling, Shawn snatched up his shirt, began to pull it on while he stamped into his boots.

"It's only Ron," Rhoda said protestingly.

"Maybe not," he replied, buckling on his gun. "My job to know for sure."

He stepped to the door, halted, looked back at the girl. Her face, set to a disapproving frown, was turned to him.

"Be out of here when I get back," he said and stepped into the dark hallway.

Rhoda's reply was a quiet laugh.

14

Starbuck moved hurriedly to the stairs, paused, a faint jingling reminding him that he still wore his spurs. Reaching down, he flipped the buckle tongues, released the straps and laid the star rowels to one side.

Continuing down the dark steps, he opened the door cautiously, and, bent low, crossed the porch, stepped in behind a thick leafed lilac at its corner.

He could see nothing of the rider. He spent a long minute probing the shadows edging the hard pack and then, still hunched, darted from the protection of the shrub to the tamarisk windbreak that formed a shield for the yard.

If the rider was Ron Hagerman he would be either in the barn or at the corral where the family horses were usually kept. Walking in short, quiet steps, keeping always in the darkness, Shawn circled the bunkhouses and other smaller structures until he came finally to the bulking shape of the barn.

Pulling up against the wall, he listened. He could hear only the faraway hooting of an owl somewhere back in the trees. If Ron was in the structure there would be sounds of movements, of gear being laid aside, of the horse shifting about. There was none of that.

Drawing his pistol, Starbuck edged toward the door at the opposite end of the wall near which he stood. An overhead moon was spreading a weak radiance upon the land, and, hugging the shadow extending from the building, he crossed to the double-width entrance.

Again he stopped, drew a deep breath and turned quickly into the wide runway. There was no one there, as he suspected, but he knew he had to be sure. Walking hurriedly down the row of stalls he came to the one where he had earlier noticed Ron's favorite horse. It was empty.

Immediately he wheeled, retraced his steps, a hard, pressing urgency pushing at him insistently. . . . One more place to look. If Ron was not there . . .

Easing quietly through the barn's entrance, he continued on in the narrow band of shadow until he gained the building's extreme corner. The corrals were only a few strides away. Again dropping into a crouch he hurried over the open stretch of ground, moved in alongside the horizontal poles of the pens. Not halting, he made his way to the one used by the family. Only Rhoda's mare was inside.

Starbuck drew himself up slowly. The rider had not been Ron Hagerman. There could be only one answer to it; the killer had come. He was having his look at the ranch, familiarizing himself with the arrangement of the yard, the location of the house, the crew's quarters and lesser buildings.

Best he return to the house — to where Price lay sleeping. There would be only a small possibility of danger for the rancher he was sure, but the killer, unaware of the precautions already taken, could decide to make his try.

Shawn took a step forward into the hushed night, checked himself abruptly as the distinct noise of dry brush raking against some passing object came to him. Instantly he moved to a small shed standing apart from the corrals, faded into its dark shadow.

Most of the yard and the entire front of the house was visible to him from that position. Gun ready, he whipped his eyes back and forth, waited. Anyone attempting to enter the structure, or moving about it, would fall within his vision.

The moments dragged by filled with only the heavy hush of the early morning hour. Now and then a weary horse stamped inside the barn or the lower corrals. The owl hooted again, a lonely, distant note floating through the silvered night. The lamp in the bunkhouse winked out and, back in the sandhills that footed the mountain, a coyote barked. But he heard no more of the intruder.

A blur of motion at the south end of the house brought him up sharply. It was the man on the horse. Starbuck spun, doubled back to the corrals, and, racing to their opposite line, cut left into the dense chamisa fringing that side of the yard.

Bent low, he walked fast and softly toward that

point. The killer had made a complete circuit of the premises, knew by that moment the location of the crew's quarters, the barn and stable, the corrals, the sheds and their relation to the main house. With such firmly in mind he had a clear picture of what Price Hagerman's pattern of movement would be.

He could visualize the rancher coming out of the house, walking across the open yard to the barn or the corrals to where his horse would be waiting. He could about guess the course he would take as he rode out onto the range — and knowing that, the killer could chose his spot and wait.

Taut, Shawn reached the last of the brush and halted. The white wall of the ranchhouse was to his left, no more than fifty feet away. Somewhere close by would be the man on his horse. The certainty of it was a strong core in his mind.

Rigid, hand gripping his six gun tightly, Starbuck listened while his straining eyes probed the pools of blackness, the lighter shadows, the moonlit aisles between the trees. The feeling within him heightened. The hair along the back of his neck prickled. . . . He was being watched. The killer knew he was there. A coldness settled over him. At that exact moment a gun was probably being leveled at him.

Instinctively he ducked low, pivoted. He whirled to one side, changing positions rapidly. A thump of quick movement to his left sent him spinning off again as realization swept him; he had been standing only a stride from the killer!

He lunged to one side as a shadow surged at him. Something solid struck his head. He was moving away however, and it was only a glancing blow. He went to hands and knees, shook his head to clear it. He hung there briefly, and then, as full awareness rushed back to him, he lunged to his feet.

The shadow was gone, the retreating sound of his horse a hurried tattoo at the end of the house. Cursing, Starbuck plunged forward through the brush, broke into the open and came to a halt behind a clump of wild rose. He swore again. The sound had faded.

He had been within reach of the killer, and the man had slipped through his hands. He shrugged, guessed he should be grateful for one thing; he had stood close to death there in the darkness. Only the intruder's reluctance to use his gun and arouse others on the ranch, and thus betray his presence, had spared him.

His attention swung into sharp focus once again as hoof beats, more distinct this time, reached him. The thud was now at the opposite end of the house. Moving quickly from the pool of shade in which he stood, Shawn ran the full length of the structure until he was once more alongside the tough, stringy windbreak.

The horseman broke into view at the end of the tamarisk, a slumped figure on his saddle outlined against the darkness. Shawn waited until he was abreast and stepped suddenly into the open.

15

Starbuck caught the headstall of the passing horse in one hand, leveled his pistol with the other.

"What the hell —"

It was Ron Hagerman. Shawn, seething inwardly at his failure to capture the killer, head aching from the glancing blow he had received, released his grip and stepped back.

"Just being sure you weren't somebody else," he said, holstering his weapon.

Ron, quieting his startled horse, came off the saddle angrily. "Who the devil'd you think I was?" he demanded.

Starbuck hooked his thumbs in his belt, studied the man coldly. "The killer you hired to put a bullet in your pa. He's come."

Hagerman's eyes flared, then narrowed quickly. He shook his head. "Don't know what you're talking about."

Shawn continued to watch him closely. "No point in playing dumb. I know all about it."

Hagerman's eyes held firm for a long moment, and then he looked away. "How'd you find out?" he asked heavily.

A faint sigh slipped through Starbuck's lips. He had hoped the story was untrue, that there was some mistake and Ron wasn't guilty of such a terrible thing; now there no longer was any doubt.

"Can't see that it makes any difference. Point is, he's here."

"You saw him?"

"Only saw a man riding a horse in the dark. He had himself a good look at the place, getting it sized up."

"And you didn't nail him?"

Impatience stirred Shawn. "Tried but I never got the chance. . . . Was him you heard leaving when you rode in."

"Never heard nobody," Ron muttered, staring off into the night. "What comes next? You telling Pa?"

Starbuck was silent in thought for a time. Finally, "Not sure — leastwise about you. Got to tell him the killer's here for certain. Need to do that so he'll be on his guard."

"Be obliged if you'll keep my part of it from him," Ron said hurriedly, coming about to face Starbuck. "Consider it a big favor."

"Yeh, expect you would. But I'm making no promises, not right now. What in the hell were you thinking of when you pulled this stunt?"

Hagerman's arms lifted and fell in a gesture of helpless frustration. "God, I don't know! I was drunk, for one thing, and plenty sore at Pa over something. You've seen how he rides me. Treats me like I was dirt under his boots."

"So when the chance turned up —"

"Was that same night —"

"— You got yourself a hired gun. Paid for him in advance."

Ron nodded woodenly.

"What's worse, you made it clear you didn't want to know who the gunslinger would be or when he'd come."

"Wanted to fix it so's I couldn't change my mind, back down. . . . Was it Rhoda who told you?"

Starbuck only shrugged. "I've talked to quite a few since I've been around."

"Had a hunch she knew," the younger Hagerman said, seemingly not hearing the reply.

"Doubt if your sister has much truck with gamblers and gunslingers," Shawn said, feeling it best to get Ron's thoughts channeled away from Rhoda. For him to know it was her who had tipped him off could accomplish nothing more than to deepen the chasm that lay between them.

Ron stirred wearily. "I'd give anything to stop it — my own life if that's the price. Like for you to believe that."

"About what it would take. You pay one of those killers to do a job and he does it, regardless. Having a one track mind is part of what it takes to be one. Who was it you got to line it up for you?"

"Gambler I knew. He used to hang around The Pack Saddle. I was in there that same night Pa and me had the big row. I must've said something about being glad when he was dead so's I could take over the ranch, run it myself, because he spoke up, told me if that was what I wanted, he could fix it for me.

"Didn't exactly understand what he meant at first and he explained. Said there were always gunmen hanging around the bigger cow towns looking to take a job like that. Said he figured to pull out that next day for Abilene, and if I wanted it done, he'd set it up for me."

"Was this idea of you not knowing who the killer would be or when he'd come yours or his?"

"His. Told me it was the way I ought to arrange it. That way nobody would know I had anything to do with it. Cost me seven hundred and fifty dollars — five hundred for the gunman, two-fifty for the gambler. I — I jumped at the chance. Was that drunk or that sore, not sure which. Anyway I made a deal and got the money to him that next day just as he was leaving town."

"How long ago?"

"About a month. Why?"

"Just wondering. About what I'd figure it would take for your killer to show up. Leaves no doubt in my mind that it was him I trailed all over the place tonight."

"Reckon we can be sure, all right," Ron murmured. "Realize I've got no right to ask, Starbuck, but you think you can head him off before he gets to Pa?"

"I'll do what I can — was what he hired me to do. Going to be a matter of waiting and watching sharp."

"You think he'll come back tomorrow?"

"Hard to say. Maybe not, after running into

115

me. More likely to wait, just hang around until everything settles down again. Want to get word passed to all the hired hands to be on the lookout for strangers."

Ron nodded. "I'll do it myself first thing in the morning."

"Start with the cook. He can spread it fast. . . . Who'll be foreman now? Guess you know Archer quit."

"Heard it in town. I don't know who. Pa'll have to find somebody."

"What's wrong with you taking over the job?"

Ron Hagerman's face reflected his surprise. "Me? Hell, you know the answer to that. Pa'd never go for the idea. He'd holler me clear off the place."

"Hollering never draws any blood, about time you realized that and maybe did some yelling right back. You figure you could handle the job?"

"Know I could — leastwise, I could run Hash Knife the way I think is right. Wouldn't be what Pa would want, though."

"Can't see as it would make much difference how you did it as long as it worked out."

"What I've tried to tell him every time we have a row over something. But I can't reach him — get it into his head. He just rides right over me, goes on doing whatever it is we're arguing about the way he wants — the way he did thirty years ago."

"Guess he believes they're the best since

they worked for him."

"Not denying that, but it's not true all the time. Like how he treats the hired hands. Drives them like they were galley slaves on one of those old ships I used to read about in school. You can't do that anymore. . . . The war changed a lot of things and that's one of them. Men nowadays are more independent. They won't take a lot of rawhiding. They'll just quit, find themselves a better job.

"Right now we don't have a single man riding the range for us who's been with Hash Knife over six months! Dave Archer was an old hand; you know how long he'd been here?"

Starbuck shook his head. This was a different Ron Hagerman than he had imagined from first impressions.

"No idea."

"A little over a year — that's all. You can't keep good help, build up loyalty by treating a crew the way Pa does."

"You ever talk to him about it — mentioning what you have to me?"

"Tried to — got nowheres fast. He won't listen to anything but what he thinks is right. If I go at him too strong, it ends up with him sending me out to do some lousy two-bit job like he did this morning. . . . That's his way of reminding me of my place."

"What about just going ahead sometime, sort of force your way?"

Ron stirred apathetically. "Be no use. Always

tried to talk, persuade him to let me handle it like I think's best. Flat out refuses me, every time. He figures I haven't got enough sense to take on any responsibility."

"There any doubt in your mind?" Starbuck asked, looking intently at Hagerman.

"No, there ain't. Plenty of things I can handle. Hell, I grew up on this ranch, know every inch of it along with all the do's and don'ts about raising beef—which I learned from him, only he won't admit it. . . . Be no sweat taking over Dave Archer's job as foreman. The crew would like it, too. I get along with them fine. And if I did he'd mighty quick find them helping and being good hands instead of just putting in time to draw wages."

"Reckon it's up to us to sell your pa on the idea, then."

"Us?"

"Seems to me you could use a little backing where he's concerned."

Ron's shoulders had come up. He peered at Shawn through the pale light. "That mean you're willing to help me — even after what I've done?"

"That killer's a different thing, something I'll have to think about and take care of. What we're talking about is a way to get you and your pa together, bring about some sort of an understanding."

"I don't know," Hagerman said in an uncertain voice. "Probably be a waste of time."

"May be, but you ought to figure it's worth the effort. . . . I gathered from talking to him that he's afraid to trust you with anything. Claims you always fell down on the jobs he gave you."

"Goddammit!" Ron exclaimed, suddenly angry. "That was ten years ago! He keeps throwing up the time when I wasn't much more than a kid twelve, fifteen years old, and didn't have much sense."

Shawn nodded. "And I expect he was judging you by himself when he was the same age —"

"Exactly what he's doing. At fifteen he was on his own, lagging for himself and already with an idea of how to get a ranch and make it big. With me, I had it already made and just waiting for me. I never had to grub for anything or worry a minute about the next day. He made it all possible — and then hates me because he did. But you can't make him see it."

"We're going to have to, somehow."

Hagerman shrugged tiredly. "No way that I can think of. He plain won't listen, unless —" Ron hesitated stared hard at Starbuck. "I know he's taken to you plenty. Might be he'd stand still for you talking to him."

"Could be, but we ought to have something special to put up to him — not just the fact that we both figure you can handle the foreman's job, that things have changed since you were fifteen. There anything coming up that's needing to be done real bad?"

Ron rubbed at his jaw, looked again into the

pale, silver night. The owl had fallen silent but now more coyotes were yapping in the hills.

"There's one thing," he said slowly. "Pa sold a little jag of steers to Evan Crockett. A thousand head. They've got to be driven to his place."

Starbuck smiled to himself. . . . A little jag of steers — a thousand head. . . . He knew of many ranches where that number would constitute the entire herd. Hagerman spoke of them as if they were barely worth mentioning.

"Not but a short drive — a couple a hundred miles, but it's through plenty rough country. Pa aims to head up the drive himself."

"Can you handle it?"

"Sure — I know I can. I wouldn't take the same trail he does because water's scarce along it and it's too hard on the cattle. That's not important to him, though; all he's interested in is delivering the stock. Might take a day longer the route I'll follow but the cattle will be in prime condition when Crockett gets them."

"I see . . . When's he figure to head out?"

"Tomorrow or the next day, last I heard."

"Good. Won't be smart for him to go riding off cross-country anyway, not with that killer hanging around. And since he's got no foreman, be the natural thing for you to take over."

"He'll never listen to it — or to what you say about the gunman, either. Bull-headed like he is, he'll go anyway."

"Maybe. I'll hit him up in the morning, tell him I think you ought to take on Archer's job

120

and handle the drive."

Ron's brows lifted, indicating his hope. "Like I said, maybe he'll listen to you. Sure won't me."

"Never be a better time than now to speak up. You've got two things going for you — the threat of that killer, and there being no foreman on the ranch."

"He won't look at it from that angle," Ron said doubt again in his tone. "He'll just remember all the things I couldn't do once, and decide right off that I'll fail again."

"We'll see. . . . One thing, when we get to talking to him about it, don't mention that you'll be doing it your way and not his. You just go ahead, take the trail you figure's best, if we convince him. Telling him about it will just be throwing more rocks in the path."

Hagerman nodded. Shawn glanced toward the house. The faint glow of lamplight against his window no longer showed.

"Come morning we'll put it up to him."

Ron Hagerman reached for the trailing reins of his horse, started to move on for the barn, halted.

"That killer . . . you decide yet whether you're going to tell Pa that I had a hand in bringing him here?"

"No . . . Something I'm still thinking over. . . . Good night."

He glanced again at the darkened window as Hagerman continued on. Rhoda, he hoped, had returned to her own bed.

16

Starbuck was the first one down and waiting in the dining room that next morning. It was by design and not accident. He wanted to step outside, have a searching look at the area around the house. The knowledge of the killer's arrival was uppermost in his mind and he knew he must take every precaution from that hour on until the gunman was either apprehended or brought down.

Shortly after he had returned from his tour of inspection and was standing by the window drinking a cup of *Mamacita's* strong coffee, Ron entered the room. He said very little other than acknowledging the greeting Shawn made, was seemingly wrapped in deep thought. Starbuck guessed he was girding himself for the battle he anticipated with Price Hagerman.

He would help Ron all he could. It meant taking it upon himself to suggest that Ron become Hash Knife's new foreman as well as being the one to head up the cattle drive to Crockett's. Once that was said, he'd go a step farther and recommend it.

Likely the rancher would resent the interference in what he considered a strict family matter — and would tell him so in plain words. But that wouldn't matter. Ron, despite the mistake he had made, deserved to be recognized and given a second chance.

Price and Rhoda came down together only moments after Ron, and all settled in their chairs. Few words other than morning salutations again seemed the rule. Rhoda, dressed for riding, did favor Shawn with a warm smile, however.

"Salazar!" Hagerman yelled, twisting about and looking toward the kitchen door. "Where's my eggs and steak?"

The squat, ever-smiling woman came into the room at once, bringing the platters of food. All had been in readiness evidently; she had simply awaited the rancher's bellowed summons.

The meal passed quickly, Shawn delaying until the final cups of coffee were poured before speaking for Ron. After that was said he would tell Price of the rider who had come in the night, go so far as to propose that he stay in the house while a search was made on the range for the rider. He doubted that Hagerman would listen, however, and —

"Pa, something I want to talk to you about."

At Ron's unexpected declaration, Starbuck glanced up. The younger Hagerman's features were taut and there was a whiteness around his cheekbones, but his voice was firm and strong. He was going to speak for himself, not permit someone else to do it for him. Shawn's estimation of the man raised another notch.

"Yeh?" Price said, leaning forward. His eyes

were filled with suspicion. "What about?"

"Me . . . and this ranch. I'm taking over the foreman job."

Hagerman rocked back in his chair. "The hell you say!"

"I'm aiming to handle the drive to Crockett's, too. Herd's ready to move. I'll head out today."

"The devil you will!" Hagerman shouted, now thoroughly aroused. "I wouldn't trust you from here to the barn with a wagonload of corn shucks!"

"You're going to have to, Pa. I'm —"

"I don't have to do a goddam thing but someday die! What made you think I'd listen to such fiddle-faddle?"

"Because I'm your son and I've got a right to be somebody on this ranch."

"You've had your chance before," Hagerman said, shaking his finger across the table. "You proved then you wasn't man enough to handle anything."

"That was years ago. I've grown up since then. You ought to realize that."

"Far as I can tell you ain't changed one whit. Be the same story was I to ever let you —"

"No, it wouldn't."

"And I'm saying it would," Hagerman shot back. "Forget it."

Ron shook his head stubbornly. "I'm doing it, Pa. I'm taking that herd to Crockett's just to prove to you that I can."

"Had all the proof I need about you."

Shawn set his empty cup back into its saucer. "Be a good idea to let Ron handle it," he said, coming into the argument. "We had a visitor last night."

Price Hagerman transferred his steady glare from his son to Starbuck. "What visitor?"

"I figure it was the man we've been waiting for."

The rancher straightened slowly. "You mean the killer who's supposed to be gunning for me?"

"Only reason I can think of for a stranger to be prowling the place at one o'clock in the morning."

"If you seen him why the hell didn't you shoot him?"

"Never got the chance. Was careful to keep out of sight."

Hagerman shrugged his annoyance, making clear he considered it another unnecessary failure. "What's that got to do with Ron moving them cattle?"

"Won't be smart for you to be out on the range."

"Forget that!" Price snapped. "I ain't crawling under the bedstead for nobody!"

"Just asking that you stay in the house —"

"Hell, no!"

Starbuck's features hardened. "You hired me to look out for you. Can't do it unless you listen to what I say."

"Then you're fired. I ain't holing up for you or anybody else."

Starbuck turned away, glanced at Rhoda, question in his eyes.

She shook her head at Hagerman. "Now, Pa, you don't mean that. You've got to do what Shawn says. It's for your own good."

"I ain't staying penned up, and that's all there is to it," the rancher declared flatly. "Never yet run from trouble, man or beast, and I'm too damned old now to start."

"Then you can't hold Starbuck responsible if something happens," Ron said.

"Ain't nothing going to happen if he's on the job like he's supposed to be."

A half smile pulled at Shawn's mouth. "Sets up quite a chore for me, the way you want it done."

"Maybe, but that's how it's going to be. Expect to go about my business same as I always do."

"And make yourself an easy target," Rhoda finished in an icy tone.

"If I do, I do. Anyway, Starbuck'll be there to stop this here killer before he can do anything."

"Unless he's standing off in the brush a hundred yards with a rifle," Shawn said quietly.

The rancher considered that. "It turns out that way," he said finally, "you won't be to blame. . . . Nobody will."

Rhoda made a small gesture with her hands. "Well, there's no need for it. All you have to do is listen to Shawn — do what he says and you'll both come out all right."

Hagerman's sharp dark eyes were on his daughter, once again appraising, assessing, drawing conclusions as to the girl and Starbuck.

"I'll take care," he said then, his manner relenting. "You worrying about him . . . or me?"

"About you, Pa."

The rancher grunted. "Yeh, I'll bet. Well, I'm heading out —"

"What about it?" Ron's voice had lost some of its firmness. "You've not given me an answer yet."

The elder Hagerman fixed his gaze on his son. "I've had my say. Ain't about to keep chewing it over and over."

"Why not? Why can't we talk it out? And how am I ever going to prove anything to you if you won't give me a chance to?"

"Don't need nothing proved — already know." Price shifted his glance to Rhoda. "What do you think, girl? You figure there's any use of it?"

"Up to you," Rhoda replied, neither backing nor opposing her brother.

Temper flared through Ron. "Why're you asking her? She's got nothing to say about it! Sure don't mean anything to her."

Price smiled quietly. "Could be she's changed, and has got more say-so than you think." Shoving back his chair he got to his feet. He stood for a bit looking down at the linen cloth, a deep frown on his face. Then, "I'll do some studying on it, give you my answer tonight."

Shawn saw surprise flood into the younger Hagerman's eyes. Evidently it was the first time he had made any headway with his father; a small victory — but a victory, nevertheless. He grinned, bobbed his head.

"Fine, Pa . . . I'll be ready to pull out in the morning — if you say so."

"All right, but don't go getting in a hurry. Said I'd think on it. Ain't saying yes to nothing, yet." He swung his attention to Shawn. "Be ready to ride in ten minutes. Got to check on Crockett's herd, see that the stock's fit to go. . . . Meet you at the corral."

Shawn rose, said, "I'll be there," in a resigned voice, and ducking his head at Rhoda and Ron, turned to go for his hat and spurs.

He had scarcely entered his room when he heard a sound behind him and wheeled. It was Rhoda. Her features were serious and concern shadowed her eyes. She looked up at him in that direct way of hers.

"Shawn . . . that stranger last night . . . do you think he's hanging around?"

"Would be my guess."

She dropped her gaze. "I . . . wish you didn't have to go out there with Pa, that he'd listen to you and stay here."

"He won't. You saw that."

"I know. . . . He's always so bull-headed."

"Taking a big chance. I'll do all I can to keep him from getting hurt."

"I know you will. What about Ron?"

He leaned over, began to buckle on his spurs. "What about him?"

"Do you think you can depend on him for help? Against the killer, I mean."

"Sure of it. And we're getting word to all the range hands to watch out for a stranger. He's sorry for what he did."

Her slim shoulders moved slightly. "A bit late for that," she murmured. "Oh, I hate him for doing it! It could mean your life. . . . And Pa's."

Starbuck, finished with the rowels, straightened slowly. His eyes searched her features closely, and then, pulling on his hat, he moved by her. In the doorway he halted, looked back.

"It's your pa you want to be worrying about," he said. "I'm nothing to you, Rhoda. Understand that. I'm just somebody passing through your life. . . . *Adios*. . . ."

17

They rode from the yard stirrup to stirrup, neither man having anything to say. A distance from the buildings Starbuck, after taking stock of the land across which they angled, dropped back and changed his position, placing himself between Price Hagerman and a low hogback of rock and stunted brush to their right.

Open country lay to the opposite side and he felt there was no danger of an ambush from that quarter; the ridge, however, offered perfect cover.

The rancher seemed not to notice the move. He was staring straight ahead, high-crowned, broad-brimmed hat tipped forward over his face, eyes vacant with deep thought. They continued on steadily, covered the first mile, and then Shawn, noting two riders in a shallow sink below them, reached out and touched Hagerman's arm.

"They some of your crew?"

Price, aroused from his reverie, peered at the men. "Expect they are. One way to find out."

Immediately he roweled the buckskin he was riding and cut directly for the pair. Starbuck, cautious, hand near the forty-five on his left hip, kept pace.

The punchers were astride horses wearing

Circle Hash Knife brands. The first, an elderly man with a hawk nose and thick mustache nodded and smiled.

" 'Morning Mister Hagerman, you looking for somebody special?"

Price shook his head. "Riding, mostly. Figured to take a look at them cattle I'm sending to Evan Crockett."

The old puncher jerked a thumb toward the south. "You'll find them in the hollow yonder side of that hill. Finished the gather yesterday. Reckon they can move out any time."

"Good."

Shawn said: "Noticed any strangers around?"

"Nope, not a one. Ron was by here a bit ago. Told us to keep our eyes peeled. Aim to do just that. . . . Your name Starbuck?"

"That's me. Been wanting to talk to you and the rest of the crew. You'd be?"

"Maury's what they call me. My friend here is Wes Lovett. It about this brother of your'n?"

Evidently Ron had passed on considerable information. "Right. Was hoping to find him working for Mr. Hagerman," Shawn said, and gave his description of Ben. "Could be calling himself Damon Friend," he finished.

The two punchers exchanged glances. Maury said, "Sure don't recollect nobody like that. . . . Name don't prod me none either."

Shawn smiled. "Obliged to you just the same. I'll be talking to the others in the next few days.

131

Might mention to them what I told you."

"Sure will do it," Maury replied, and, settling back on his saddle, watched Hagerman and Starbuck ride on.

The rancher, frowning, was staring at Shawn. There was an odd, quizzical look in his eyes. "You hear what he said about Ron — that he'd already been by here?"

"Expect he got a quicker start than we did. Know from last night he was planning to get word about the killer passed to the crew."

Hagerman swore wonderingly. "Just can't figure that. Was in my mind that he was at the house, crawled back into bed and sleeping. What he usually does when he's been out half the night whoring around."

"You know that for sure or are you just guessing?"

"Damn it — I know! It's what he's always done."

Starbuck's shoulders lifted, fell. "That's where all the trouble between you two lays. It's what he used to do. Not that way now, but you keep judging him by the past."

"I know what I know, and he —"

"You two'll never get together unless you start looking at the Ron that's your son today. He's changed. He's different — a full grown man."

Hagerman studied Shawn narrowly. "You're mighty certain for a fellow who's only known him a couple of days."

"Makes it easy. I'm a stranger, an outsider. I

can see it, and I'm pretty well acquainted with the problem. Turns up in about every family like yours."

"Ain't sure I'm liking the sound of that."

"Most of the time the truth does have a saw-tooth edge. Can hurt like hell — and that means plenty of folks dodge it."

"The truth that's hurting me," the rancher said with a shrug, "is that my own flesh and blood ain't worth a bucket of tick-dip."

"That's where you're wrong maybe. You won't give Ron a chance to prove it — something he wants to do so bad he —" Starbuck let the words die off, unwilling to go any farther. Ron was guilty of a terrible deed, but he still couldn't bring himself around to telling Price Hagerman of it.

The rancher waited for him to finish, and when he did not, prompted: "He'd what?"

"Take on most anything to make you see it — like wanting the foreman job, and driving that herd you've sold to whoever it was that bought it."

Hagerman shifted wearily. "I just ain't got no confidence in the boy —"

"He's not a boy! He's older than I am. Whole trouble is you've lost touch with each other. You talk the same language, only it's not on the same level." Shawn paused, grasping for words with which he could make Price Hagerman understand.

The rancher was a breath ahead of him.

"Reckon I see what you're trying to say. There just ain't no connection running between us. It's like being joined by a rope only there's a knot in the middle neither one of us can get around."

"You're putting it better than I can."

Hagerman brushed at his jaw. "Well, don't you get the idea I like it! God knows I want my son to be the man I've always hoped for."

"Only answer to that is for you to give him an opportunity —"

"Expect when you come right down to it, that's the big problem. I'm plain scared to let him try — scared he'll fall down on me again like he's always done before, and I don't think I can swallow that another time."

"Which is the wrong way to feel about it," Starbuck said, looking out over the flat now warming rapidly to the touch of the sun.

He glanced again to the hogback. The course they were following had veered nearer to it. Imperceptibly, he began to alter direction, force the rancher's buckskin more to the south, thus place more ground between them and the rocks.

"You'll never know if Ron can come up to your expectations unless you let him try. . . . You're just closing the book on him, saying he can't without really knowing."

Hagerman was silent for a long time. Finally: "Maybe it is my fault. Maybe me being scared of him failing is what the big trouble is."

Shawn nodded to the older man, smiled. He realized what it took for Price Hagerman to make that admission. "You're on the right track now."

"What's the answer? What ought I do?"

"I'd start off letting Ron head up that trail drive. Might cost you some steers if things don't pan out exactly right, but you'd at least know — both of you."

"Hell, cattle don't mean nothing to me. I'd give Crockett the whole damned herd for free if it would help any. Be rough on him, however. It's a mean trip. Had plenty of trouble myself making it last time."

"All the better. Ron comes through it without losing a lot of cattle, you'll both be satisfied."

"Yeh, reckon that's right. . . . You be willing to ride along, sort of help him out in case he gets in over his head?"

Starbuck shook his head. "Be the worst thing you could do, having me go with him. You've both got something to prove; you that you've got faith in him, and he that he can do the job. You send me he'll know right away that you don't trust him and think he still needs looking after."

Again a stillness came over the rancher. Larks were skimming over the short grass, wheeling and dipping, pausing to alight now and then on a clump of weeds or a rotting stump. In the clean sky overhead crows straggled brokenly for the ranch and the feed they knew could be found around the corrals.

"All right," Hagerman said abruptly, pulling his horse to a stop. "I'm going to do it. I'm telling him tonight it's his job, and if he can do it he'll take over Archer's saddle and run the whole damned she-bang."

Shawn grinned. "And I'm laying odds you won't regret it. About time you started taking it easy, anyway."

"For a fact! Been pounding leather day in and day out for a lot of years. . . . You know, never would admit it to myself, but I've been sort of looking forward to —"

A faint, hollow crack sounded in the warm hush. Price Hagerman stiffened. A strange, puzzled look crossed his face as he raised a hand to his chest.

Starbuck reacted instantly. He lunged from the sorrel, caught the rancher around the waist and dragged him from his horse.

"Keep low!" he shouted, drawing his gun and pivoting as the rifle spoke again.

18

Starbuck threw himself forward, went flat on his belly. Steadying himself on his elbows, he squeezed off two quick shots. He had only a puff of smoke arising from a ragged clump of brush along the hogback for a target. The killer had chosen his position well.

A stir of movement behind the weedy growth caught Shawn's eye. He triggered a third bullet. The clatter of metal upon rock came faintly to him — the sound, perhaps, of a rifle being dropped. Starbuck grinned tightly. He had scored, but how badly hurt the bushwhacker was he could only guess. Rolling to one side, he rodded out the spent cartridges in the cylinder of his pistol and reloaded.

He heard the hoof beats of oncoming horses approaching from the south, turned to look. Three riders. Hash Knife men who had heard the shooting and were moving in to investigate. Holstering his weapon, he swung about to Price Hagerman. The rancher lay on his back, a hand pressed to a flowing wound in his chest.

"Got me . . . pretty good . . . seems," the older man muttered.

Starbuck jerked off his bandana, folded it into a pad, and lifting the rancher's fingers, placed it against the wound.

"Hold that there — tight. I'll get you back to the house."

He rose to his feet, faced the riders pounding to a stop before them. "Over there — behind that biggest juniper," he said, pointing toward the hogback. "Think I put a bullet into him but I'm not sure. . . . Don't let him get away!"

The men nodded, spurred off. Starbuck knelt beside the rancher, took him under the armpits and helped him to his feet. He had a bit of difficulty with the buckskin but finally Hagerman was on the saddle. Shawn mounted at once, and, taking the reins of the man's horse, struck for the ranch.

Off to his left he could see the riders closing in on the cedar. Sunlight glinted on their guns, and as he watched all halted abruptly. They seemed to listen for a few moments and then, as one, they rode over the crest of the ridge and disappeared beyond. . . . It could mean but one thing; the killer had fled and they were giving chase. His bullet had missed its mark after all — or else had inflicted only a minor wound.

Price Hagerman was having trouble staying on his horse. He gripped the horn with both hands, swayed back and forth brokenly even at the slow pace Shawn had set. As they reached the rise to the west of the ranch, he almost toppled from the saddle.

Starbuck, fearing such would occur, halted at once. Dropping from the sorrel, he turned to the buckskin and swung up behind the suffering rancher. Encircling him with an arm and holding firmly, he gripped the leathers in his free hand and dug spurs into the horse. The buckskin was not big enough to carry double for any distance, but they were almost home and that worried him little.

Rhoda saw them when they entered the yard. She crossed to the edge of the porch, stared, turned quickly back to the doorway.

"*Mamacita!* Pa's been hurt!" the girl cried into the house.

She came off the gallery then, hurried to meet them. Behind her the screen slammed as the Mexican woman ran into the open. Shawn did not halt but continued on until he was opposite the entrance. Rhoda, keeping pace at the buckskin's flank, looked up at him anxiously.

"Is it bad?"

Starbuck nodded as he swung down. "Get somebody going for the doctor."

The girl whirled away, ran toward the crew's quarters. *Mamacita* Salazar, dark face sober, stood at the door holding it wide.

"There is a bed —" she began, pointing to her left.

Shawn, gathering the rancher in his arms, headed for the stairway. "Better for him to be in his own."

"But the steps, *señor* —"

"I can make it. Bring some hot water, and rags for bandages."

The woman scurried off toward the kitchen.

Halfway up the stairs he heard Rhoda enter and rush to assist him.

"Go on," he said. "Get things ready for him."

Lips tight, she moved ahead of him. "I've sent for the doctor."

Starbuck gained the upper floor, carried the wholly quiet Hagerman into his room and placed him on his bed. The rancher's contorted face was beaded with sweat and a sallowness had replaced the weathered brown of his skin. At once Shawn began to remove the man's shirt. Rhoda worked to take off his boots.

Mrs. Salazar appeared, a steaming kettle in one hand, a quantity of clean, white cloths in the other. She hustled Starbuck aside, bent over the rancher to examine the ugly, puckered hole in his chest from which a steady trickle of blood flowed.

Shawn felt Rhoda's fingers grip his wrist. "Is . . . is he —"

"He lives," *Mamacita* cut in before Starbuck could reply. "But it will be good if the doctor comes soon."

Folding a strip of cloth, she dipped it into the hot water, squeezed it almost dry and began to clean away the crusted blood surrounding the wound.

"He looks so pale . . . and he doesn't move or make a sound," Rhoda murmured.

"It was a rifle bullet. They hit a man plenty hard. He's in sort of a coma from it."

A small sound of desperation escaped the

girl's lips. "Isn't there something we can do? I —"

"Go — I will care for him!" Mrs. Salazar broke in, jerking her head at the door. "I will call if there is need. . . . Go — now!"

Shawn took Rhoda's arm, steered her into the hallway and down the stairs.

"There'll be coffee on the stove," she said when they had reached the lower floor.

Starbuck followed her into the kitchen, sat down at the oil-cloth covered table in the center of the room while she poured a cup for each. When she had settled onto her chair, she looked directly at him, her eyes frank and steady.

"How did it happen?"

"Somebody was hiding along that ridge below here. Was afraid of the place — all that brush and rock made it a good spot for an ambush. . . . Tried to keep it at a distance."

"Whoever it was — did you see him?"

"Got only a look at something moving. Threw a bullet into it and I thought I heard a gun bang into the rocks like it had been dropped. Maybe nothing to it, though. Three of the crew showed up and I sent them over for a look. He was gone when they got there."

Starbuck stared moodily into his cup, swished the dark liquid about slowly. "Should have made your pa stay here — in the house. . . . Might've known this would happen."

"Don't blame yourself. You couldn't have kept him here unless you roped him down. Do

141

you think it was the man you saw last night?"

"Probably. No way of knowing for sure — yet."

Lifting the cup, he took a long swallow. A disturbing thought had crept into his mind, one he did not like to consider. Setting the cup in its saucer, he said:

"Has Ron been back? He was out there ahead of us. . . . Expect he ought to be told what's happened."

The underlying meaning of the question was not lost to Rhoda. Aware of the deal he had made for a gunman, it was only natural that she glide to a conclusion.

"Do you think it was Ron who did it — ambushed Pa?"

Starbuck shrugged, regretting now that by his words he had planted the idea in her mind.

"Sort of doubt that it was him."

But he was not entirely convinced himself. Ron had seemed to change, become more reconciled to a reasonable approach where his problems with Price Hagerman were concerned, but later, frustration and anger could have taken over again. He could have concluded that proceeding on such basis was hopeless and settled with himself for a more direct and immediate method. . . . It came suddenly to Shawn that he did not actually know Ron Hagerman well enough to judge; the son could be everything the father declared him to be.

"Your pa had just decided to let him handle

that cattle drive to Crockett's when the bullet hit him. Said, too, that if he made good at it, he was to be the new foreman."

Rhoda, coffee yet untouched, looked away, gaze reaching through the window to the yard beyond. Two men were speaking with the cook in front of the kitchen shack, a third was moving up from the bunkhouse. Evidently, word of Price Hagerman's shooting had spread fast.

"Poor Ron," she murmured. "He's always doing the wrong thing at the wrong time. . . . I expect you had something to do with Pa changing his thinking."

"Not specially," Starbuck replied, shifting about on his chair. "We just talked. He made up his own mind."

"Of course. That's the way he is — never really listens to anybody. . . . Shawn . . . if anything happens to him, what will I do?"

"Just go right on living and doing the same as other folks have to do when somebody dies. Ron can run this ranch — and you can help. Can't see as there would be any big change for you. But don't count your pa out yet. He's bad hurt, but he's a tough one."

She was only half listening. "I . . . I don't know about Ron. There's never been much between us. He'd resent me, I'm sure, and if I thought he was the one who'd hid along the ridge — and knowing he had hired that killer, too, I couldn't stay around him. I'd hate him too much."

"Don't brand him with that bushwhacking

yet. Good chance it was the killer, not him. Far as the other goes, he's walking through hell bare-footed regretting it. He was drunk and mad both when he did it — and I'm pretty sure he'd die keeping that killer from getting to your pa if he could."

Rhoda frowned. "Then you don't blame him —"

"Sure I do! No excuse for a stunt like that, sore and drunk or not. But anybody can make a mistake. Some make worse ones than others. That's the kind he's made — the worst there is. He admits it and he'd do anything to call it back."

"Mistakes," she said quietly, woodenly. "Guess we'd all like to change some of the things we've done. . . . If it turns out bad for Pa, is there a chance you can stay around, at least for awhile?"

He considered that for a time. Then, "I signed on for a month, Rhoda. When that's finished I'll have to move on. I —"

Shawn hesitated as a quick hush of hooves sounded in the yard. Rising quickly, he glanced through the window.

"It's Ron," he said and wheeled to the door.

19

Ron Hagerman's features were strained as he entered the house. He saw Shawn and Rhoda waiting just inside the room, pulled up.

"Pa . . . is he —"

"Alive," Starbuck said. "We're waiting on the doctor."

Ron moved on, mounted the stairs hurriedly and crossed to his father's room. Shawn stepped to the entrance, glanced out. Hagerman's horse, reins dragging where he had been hastily abandoned, was directly in front of the house. A rifle was in the saddle boot. Starbuck shook his head at the thought nesting in his mind. It meant nothing. There were very few riders who didn't pack a long gun on the range. He turned, aware that Rhoda was at his shoulder.

"You're not sure that it wasn't him after all, are you?"

"Not certain of anything," he said grudgingly. "I've still got my doubts. . . . That doctor ought to be showing up, seems."

"Be awhile yet. Are you going to ask Ron?"

"Ask me what?"

Hagerman, thin lipped and features drawn, had descended the stairs quietly, was now only a step behind them. Rhoda's eyes flashed defiantly.

"If it was you who shot Pa!"

Ron's head came up angrily. "You think I could have done that —" he began, and then his shoulders sagged. "I guess you've got a right to."

"Was it?" the girl persisted.

"No," Ron said in a low voice.

Shawn considered him narrowly. "You hear the shots?"

The younger Hagerman stirred helplessly. "No."

"Understood from a couple of the crew we ran into that you were there ahead of us."

"Expect I was. Was riding over for a look at Crockett's herd and to get word to the men about that killer while I was doing it. Went far as the line shack on Mule Creek, then cut back to the west range."

"Still seems to me you could have heard the shooting," Rhoda said quietly.

"Well, I didn't!" Ron replied, face hardening. "You hear it?"

"No, of course not. I was —"

"About the same distance. You've got no more right to think I should have heard it than I have of you —"

"Not important now," Starbuck cut in, putting an end to the senseless wrangling. "How was he?"

"Like he was dead. Just lays there hardly breathing. How did it happen?"

"We were riding along below that hogback —"

"I know where. One of the boys told me that.

Like to know how."

Shawn related the incident, completed it by saying that three of the crew had given chase to the bushwhacker and were yet to return.

"When they get back — and if they had some luck — we ought to have the answers to several things."

Ron's glance met Starbuck's, held. "And if they don't run him down it's going to look all the more to you like it was me, that the way of it?"

"I figure the truth will come out, no matter what," Shawn replied, evenly.

Rhoda, still bristling, said, "Here's something that ought to make you proud of yourself — Pa had decided you would make the trail drive to Crockett's."

Hagerman stared at his sister. "He tell you that?"

"Told Shawn. Also said that if you did the job right you'd take over as ranch foreman."

Ron stood mute and disbelieving.

Starbuck said, "Something else that doesn't make much difference now. You'll have to head up the drive, same as you're now running Hash Knife."

"Guess that's so. It hadn't come to me yet. What does is that Pa was going to let me do it, and that's a big thing to me." He hesitated, looked squarely at Shawn. "Guess I've got you to thank for it."

"We just talked it over. Don't give me a lot of credit I don't deserve."

Hagerman glanced at Rhoda, then back to Starbuck. "That other thing — the hired killer — did you tell him?"

"No."

Rhoda frowned. "Are you going to?"

"We'll see. Right now I don't figure there's a need to. Damage has been done, and feeling the way your pa does about Ron for maybe the first time in his life, I wouldn't want to tear it all down for him."

"Pa wouldn't want it that way," Rhoda declared firmly. "He'd prefer knowing. He's always been strong for being honest and straight talk."

"On most things, I expect he would. This is different — like telling a man he's going to die. There's times when it's best to keep quiet about it."

Rhoda continued to frown. "I think you're wrong —"

"Leave it up to me," Starbuck said, his tone almost a command. "I'll do the right thing when the moment comes."

Ron nodded. "I know you will, and whatever you decide to is all right with me. . . . I'll tell him myself if you think it's what I should do."

"No, leave it to me," Starbuck repeated. "Rhoda, have I got your word on it?"

The girl's shoulders moved slightly. She had changed again it appeared to Shawn, was now filled with a hard bitterness and displaying a hatred for her brother.

"Whatever you say," she murmured, and, wheeling, headed for the stairway.

Ron watched her go in thoughtful silence. "Guess Pa means more to her than I figured — and me even less. But that's my fault. Never once tried to be a brother to her — or even know her. I can understand the way she feels toward me, and I can't blame her."

"She surprises me, too," Starbuck said. "But down deep I think your pa and you — even the ranch — mean plenty to her. A lot of that hell-I-don't-care manner of hers is just show."

"Only hope he pulls through. Like to try making it up to both of them — be what I should have been all these years."

"Not all your fault. . . . Best way you can start is to get that herd of cattle to Crockett's without any slip-up. That'll be proof to both of them."

"You think I ought to go ahead, start the drive in the morning?"

"Up to you — and maybe depends a lot on what the doc says when he gets here."

"Can tell you right now how Pa will look at it. He'll order me to go on. He told Crockett the herd would be there by the first of the month and he believes in keeping his word. I'd have to start tomorrow to make it in time."

Shawn gave that thought. "He'll be wanting you to make good on his promise, no doubt of that," he said after a bit. "But let the doctor do the deciding for you. He may figure it best you stick around close. If you're a few days late

Crockett'll understand when he learns the reason for it."

A shout went up at the lower end of the yard. Starbuck wheeled. A half a dozen riders were coming into the cleared ground near the bunkhouses. A man was draped over the saddle of a seventh horse.

"They've got him," he said, stepping out onto the hard pack. He glanced at Ron. "Sorry for what I was thinking."

"Forget it," Hagerman said.

The riders, now surrounded by a dozen more men — night crew members routed out of their sleep by the yelling — pulled to a halt near the porch.

"He's dead," one of the men said soberly. "We trailed him from the rocks. Was hit all right. . . . You got him in the leg."

"He seen us a following," another added. "Holed up in them buttes south of the creek. We was hoping he'd come peaceable but he had a mind to make a fight of it. Something we sure didn't figure on him doing."

"Couldn't be helped," Starbuck said. "Any of you get hurt?"

"Amos Whitfield. Caught hisself a slug in the leg."

"Doc's on his way here now to look after Pa. He can take care of Amos, too," Ron said.

"Fine. . . . How is the mister?"

"Pretty bad shape," Hagerman replied, and moved to where the blanketed shape lay across its saddle. Taking the edge of the cover he raised it. "Anybody know who he is?"

"Know him?" one of the riders echoed. "Why, it's Dave Archer! Figured you knowed!"

Ron had turned, was staring at Starbuck. Shawn, as if unable to believe it, stepped up to the horse and had his look. Behind him Hagerman's dragging voice could be heard.

"Then . . . the killer . . . he's still on the loose."

Starbuck turned to face him. "The way it adds up. Archer was a man with a grudge and tried to settle it. But it means that gunslinger's still hanging around."

20

Starbuck watched the riders wheel slowly away, move off onto the road leading to Brasada with Dave Archer's lifeless body. Ira Blackburn would be paying Hash Knife a call before sundown, they could all be sure of that.

"Think maybe you're wrong," Ron said, breaking into his consciousness. "Be no need for that killer to wait around now."

"You're forgetting something," he replied. "Odds are good he won't know anything about Archer shooting your pa. He's laying out in the brush somewhere, dodging everybody. Word will never get to him. We'll play it safe, keep on expecting him."

"Suppose you're right," Hagerman said, and turned to re-enter the house. He halted, seeing Rhoda standing in the doorway, her gaze on the departing riders.

"Ought to satisfy you," he said with no particular heat. "There's your proof it wasn't me that put a bullet in Pa."

"I heard," she said, and faced him. There was a glitter of tears in her eyes. "I'm glad I was wrong."

"Like to believe that —"

The dry slicing noise of iron tires cutting into sand reached Shawn. He swung his attention from the Hagermans to the road leading up to the yard. A light buggy drawn by a lathered horse was rounding the windbreak.

"This the doctor?" he asked, breaking the hush that had fallen between Ron and Rhoda.

Hagerman nodded. "That's him. Old Henry Dice. He's not much but he's all we've got around here."

The physician hauled up at the edge of the porch, flung the reins at Shawn and climbed down. He was an elderly man, as well along in years as Price Hagerman, but there was a sharpness in his glance and a steadiness in his manner that denied time.

"Where is he?" he demanded briskly, grabbing a satchel from under the seat.

"Upstairs —"

"Upstairs," Dice repeated, brushing by Starbuck. He touched the girl with a look. "Rhoda, I'll be needing you. Mrs. Salazar still around? Good. She'll have to help, too."

Shawn waited until the medical man, trailed by Rhoda, had entered the house, and then, wrapping the leathers around the whipstock, led the still heaving horse into the shade of nearby trees. Making use of the iron tether ball lying on the floor of the buggy, he retraced his steps to the porch. Ron had not stirred, was staring vacantly into the house.

Starbuck touched him on the arm, pointed at the chairs on the gallery. "Might as well sit. . . . Nothing we can do except wait."

153

It was a good two hours later when Henry Dice thumped tiredly down the steps and moved toward the porch. Ron, rising quickly, met him as he pushed open the screen.

"How is he?"

The doctor pursed his lips, shrugged. "Bad. No point in not telling you. I got the bullet out, but he lost a hell of a lot of blood — and he's not a young buck anymore."

Shawn, stepping in behind Hagerman, said, "That mean he's liable not to make it?"

"Hard to tell. Price is tough as a boot, but like I said, he's old and there's plenty against him."

"He'll come through it," Ron stated, nodding his head. "Nothing'll get Pa down."

Dice gave the younger Hagerman a speculative look. "Could be — but I wouldn't do too much planning on it. What he needs now is rest and quiet. Expect you to see that he gets it. I've done all I can for the time being. Be back tomorrow unless you send for me sooner."

The physician stepped off the gallery and walked heavily to where Shawn had parked his buggy. The minutes he had spent wrestling for Price Hagerman's life had taken much out of him, showed him now for what he was — a tired, worn-out old man.

"Pa's asking for you — both of you," Rhoda said from the doorway.

Both men wheeled at once, followed her up the stairway. Half-way up Ron slowed his step.

"You figure it's all right? From the way Dice talked he —"

"The doctor gave him something to ease the pain and make him sleep. He's awfully weak, but he kept saying he had to see you."

Starbuck hung back when they reached the rancher's room. Hagerman opened his eyes as Ron entered. He was pale, looked sunken and the appearance of bigness was gone from him.

"Boy," he said in a low, husky voice, "want you to take that herd to Crockett."

Ron nodded. "Aim to start in the morning."

"See that you do. . . . Was figuring to tell you at supper time. Had made up my mind. . . . Getting shot didn't have nothing to do with it."

"I know, Pa. Starbuck told me. . . . Don't worry, I can handle it fine — same as I can handle the place when I get back."

"You want Starbuck to go with you?"

"If you say so. Won't need him, however. I think it's best he stay here, sort of look after things for me until I return."

"Suit yourself," Price Hagerman said drowsily, and, drawing his hand from beneath the light coverlet, extended it to Ron. "Luck . . . son."

The younger man looked down hastily. He moved forward, took the limp fingers into his own, pressed them. "Thanks, Pa," he mumbled and turned away.

Mamacita Salazar, standing impatiently by, a disapproving frown clouding her dark features,

155

bobbed her head briskly.

"It is good," she said. "Now you will all go. The *patron* must sleep. The doctor say so. . . . I will stay. *Go.*"

Rhoda came about slowly, followed her brother from the room. Seeing Starbuck just outside the door, she moved to him, caught his arm.

"He's going to die, Shawn . . . I . . . I know," she cried softly.

The tall rider slipped his arm about her shoulders, continued on for the stairs. Ron, eyes fixed straight ahead, was already halfway down.

"Don't give up on him yet," Starbuck said. "His kind never quits easy."

There was a small room on the ground floor that had been used as quarters for the cook in the days when the Hagermans had both a housekeeper and a woman to take care of the kitchen chores.

Starbuck transferred his belongings that same night. The belief that danger from the killer was far from past still occupied his mind, and, thus convinced, he felt the need to be in a position where he would have a command of not only the entrance to the house but of the yard as well.

There had been no further sign of the intruder, nor had there been any reports from the crew of strangers in the area, but to Shawn this was no assurance. The reputation of a hired killer in the circle wherein he moved depended upon the thoroughness with which he accomplished the task he contracted to do. Therefore, Shawn was certain the man would not back off until he either completed his chore or had proof that Price Hagerman was dead.

But as the tension-filled days dragged slowly by, during which the rancher fought a stubborn battle toward recovery, Starbuck did have the satisfaction of seeing to his own mission. He talked with each member of the crew as they came in off the range — and learned nothing of value.

All had been riding for Hash Knife a relatively short time, no more than half a year in most cases, and none could recall any man fitting Ben's description or that had answered to the name of Damon Friend.

It was the cook, Charley Hubbs, who came up finally with a lone possibility. Hubbs had worked for Price Hagerman for a bit more than a year. There had been a man, he recalled, who had quit shortly after he signed on for the kitchen job — one who had ridden for Hagerman almost three years and was somewhat of a celebrity because of it.

His name, Hubbs recalled after considerable pondering, had been Jim Winfield. (According to the dates Shawn had mentioned, he would have been working for Hash Knife at the same time); thus he would probably be the only person likely to know if there had ever been a Damon Friend on the spread.

It wasn't much to go on, but the leads Shawn dug up usually weren't, and he was now more or less inured to disappointment. Thus, when he turned to Rhoda that evening at the supper table for additional information, he wasn't too hopeful.

"A Jim Winfield," he said, after hearing from her that Price seemed much improved — had even sat up for a time during the day. "He worked for you quite awhile. Quit about a year ago. You remember him?"

Rhoda gave it thought. She had matured much in the past few days, was far different from the girl he had encountered upon arrival.

"Name doesn't sound familiar. Why?"

"He would have been around at about the same time as my brother — if Ben was ever here."

"I see. But if he's gone now —"

"I'll try to locate him. Chance he could tell me where Ben headed after leaving Hash Knife."

"If, as you say, your brother was here."

"Something I won't know unless I find this Winfield and talk to him."

Rhoda smiled wanly. "Which makes it two men that you have to track down. Seems a bit hopeless to me."

"Way it goes sometimes. . . . You sure you don't remember him?"

"I'm sure. Never have paid much attention to the help. Even if I did, I'd have no idea what happened to him. Riders just come and go — show up from nowhere, disappear into nowhere. Maybe Ron can tell you something about him. . . . Or you could ask around town."

"Be what I'll do if Ron doesn't remember. Glad your pa's coming along."

"He's better, but he's still weak. That's what worries me — *Mamacita,* too. He can't get his strength back."

"Takes time. Little surprised he's doing as well as he is. What does the doc say?"

"That he's making progress — nothing more than that. Doesn't mean a thing far as I'm concerned. It's just something to use as an answer. . . . He asks about you every once in awhile."

"Like to go up and talk to him soon as you think it's all right. Did look in through the door a couple of times. Was asleep."

"That's what he does most of the time. I think what he needs is something to perk him up, stir his interest. I'm beginning to think he doesn't really care whether he gets well or not."

Starbuck pushed back from the table. "Doesn't sound like him. It be all right if I pay a call in the morning? Maybe I can help a little."

"I wish you would . . . and don't pay any attention to *Mamacita* if she fusses at you. Your coming can't do him any harm. Do you still think that killer will show up?"

"Pretty sure he will."

"Pa asked about him several times, too. He still wonders who it was that hired him."

Shawn glanced sharply at her. "You didn't tell him?"

Rhoda shook her head. "No . . . I gave you my word I wouldn't. I'll keep it. But don't you think he may have given up and ridden on?"

"Not the way he'd do. And when he finally comes I've got to be expecting him. . . . You don't get two chances with his kind."

21

Late that next day, with the breathless heat grip-ping the land relentlessly, a rider pounded into the yard.

Starbuck, hunched in the shade of a cotton-wood a few strides from the front of the house, recognized the man as Wes Lovett, one of the pair he had met that first morning when Price Hagerman was shot and who later had gone with Ron on the drive.

Brushing away the sweat on his face, and im-mediately worried, Shawn rose and crossed to the rack where the puncher had halted.

"Something wrong?"

Lovett grinned at him. "Nope — the other way around. I got to see Mr. Hagerman."

Starbuck glanced to the doorway. Rhoda, at-tracted by the hoof beats, was standing there looking questioningly toward them.

"Ron sent you, that it?" Starbuck said.

Lovett bobbed his head. "Said I was to see the old man — I mean, Mr. Hagerman."

Again Shawn looked to Rhoda. "It's all right," she said. "I think he's awake."

Starbuck led the rider into the house, and, ac-companied by Rhoda, conducted him to the rancher's bedroom. Earlier he had paid his call on Price, had found him indifferent and listless, as the girl had said.

"Got a visitor for you," he announced, pushing the young puncher up to the foot of the bed. "Says Ron sent him."

"Yes, sir, Mr. Hagerman, he sure did. I'm Wes Lovett."

The rancher stirred, frowned. "Lovett? You one of the crew?"

"Yes, sir. Been with Ron on the drive. He wanted you to know everything went real good. We never lost a single cow — no, sir — not one!"

"That so?" Hagerman said, pulling himself up slightly. Rhoda stepped forward at once, braced his back with a pillow.

"Not a head lost," the rancher repeated. "That sure is mighty fine."

"Ron figures to be home tomorrow, had me come on ahead so's you'd know how he made out."

Price Hagerman was nodding, showing his pleasure. A tinge of color was filtering into his sallow cheeks and the brightness in his eyes had increased.

"I appreciate your hurrying back to tell me, Wes Lovett. Was a kind thing to do."

"Was Ron's idea. Said he was anxious for you to hear about it. . . . Well, I'd best be going."

"Obliged to you again," Hagerman murmured, smiling as the rider hurried from the room and clomped down the stairs.

"Best medicine I could've got," he said then, shifting his eyes to Shawn and Rhoda. "Makes me plumb proud, knowing what the boy done. Reckon there ain't no doubt now about him."

Rhoda leaned over, wiped the beads of sweat from his brow. "You were right to give him his chance, Pa. I'm glad you did."

The rancher looked closely at her. "You mean that? You saying it from your heart?"

She nodded. "I am, Pa. Guess we've all learned a few things in the past days."

"Ain't no doubt of that, either," Hagerman said.

Strength seemed to be flowing into the man from some unsuspected source. He pulled himself to a sitting position, placed his gaze on Starbuck.

"Asking a favor of you. I'm plenty damned sick of this bed. Like to have you tote me downstairs, let me set out on the porch. Reckon you can do that?"

"Pa —" Rhoda began, protestingly.

"Now, don't go fighting me over it. Can rest as cozy there as I can here — better maybe. Won't be so goddam hot, and I've took a notion I'd like to see how things are looking."

Price Hagerman was beginning to sound like his old self again. Shawn glanced to the girl. She shrugged.

"I guess there's no harm — and it will be cooler." She smiled, waggled a finger at the rancher. "One thing, you're coming in at sundown — and no argument. . . . I won't have you overdoing it."

"Overdoing it!" Hagerman scoffed. "Ain't no man ever overdone anything yet by just setting, far as I know."

Rhoda made no reply. She gathered up one of the quilts and the two pillows, nodded to Starbuck and headed for the door. Shawn moved the rancher to the edge of the bed, slipped his arms under the man's body and lifted him. Faint surprise ran through him. In the few days Price Hagerman had been confined to his room, he had dwindled to a mere shell.

Mrs. Salazar appeared at that moment, showing her great displeasure of the idea, but she quailed before the rancher's glare, and, stepping ahead, held back the door and assisted in making him comfortable in one of the big chairs on the gallery.

Settled, Hagerman waved both Rhoda and the elderly woman off. "Ain't no sense fussing over me now. Go on about your business. I got some talking to do with Starbuck."

The rancher's voice again dragged, and some of the color had faded from his cheeks, bespeaking the toll of his strength the move had taken. Shawn, watching him closely, wondered if it would not have been better to deny his wish, then decided it would make little difference. Likely, any pleasure Price Hagerman took now was on borrowed time.

"Feels right, just setting here looking and seeing things," the rancher said after the women had disappeared into the house. "Seems to me now I never took time for such."

Starbuck moved to the edge of the porch, swept the edge of the yard with a sharp gaze. Hagerman was an easy target there in his chair, and that realization set his nerves to points, stirred a worry within him. If the killer chose this hour to make his play he could easily — with a rifle — accomplish his purpose from the shelter of the brush beyond the yard.

"Makes me kind of warm inside, knowing Ron's going to be all right," Hagerman continued, his words slow and spaced. "Wondering now about that gal of mine. There anything between the two of you?"

Starbuck drifted slowly down the length of the porch to its end where he could have a closer look at the side of the house.

"No, afraid not."

"Too bad. . . . Sure wish't there was. You and Ron taking over Hash Knife would be a fine thing for you both."

"Know that. Expect a man couldn't ask for better, but the day won't come when I can settle down until I find my brother. Once that's behind me, I can think about a wife and a home."

Hagerman was thoughtful for a full minute. Then, "Just don't wait too long, son. Take a little advice from me — don't let your life get away from you. It can mighty easy. I'm seeing that now."

"Some things a man has to do."

"Sure. Felt that way myself," the rancher said,

his eyes traveling slowly over the yard, the buildings, the flats beyond. "Know now I should have taken a bit of time for living. . . . Sun just come up and went down every day. I was so dang busy doing what I thought was needful that I never even noticed it."

Hagerman paused, reached for the light quilt Rhoda had draped about him, masked a spasm of coughing with a corner.

"Talking's not resting," Shawn said, frowning.

The rancher dismissed the protest with a wave of his hand. "Missed the sun these last few days when I was laid up and couldn't see it. Same as I missed a lot of other things — little things like stopping by the creek for a cool drink, and watching quail run and setting a horse with saddle leather rubbing the insides of my legs. . . .

"Seems a lot of things I plain overlooked — but I reckon the biggest was letting my own flesh and blood grow up with me paying them no mind. I just let it happen — but a man gets hisself so caught up in what he's doing that he forgets there's others around. . . . I sure wish't their ma hadn't died. They'd had her, maybe things wouldn't have been so hard for them."

Again Price Hagerman broke into a rash of coughing. Rhoda appeared in the doorway, alarm tightening her features. The rancher managed a grin, winked broadly at her.

"Choking on my own damned spit!"

The girl smiled back, touched Shawn with her

glance and disappeared.

"Watched you tramping back and forth like a shyster waiting on a jury. You still expecting that killer to show up?"

Starbuck nodded. "He'll have to be reckoned with. Nothing's changed there."

Hagerman laughed quietly, coughed, laughed again. "Joke's sure on him if he does. Another man's gone and done his job for him. . . . One thing, I'm kind of anxious to know who hates me so bad he'd pay to get me killed."

Starbuck swept the brush once again in a careful probe. The day was beginning to end. In a short time the sun would drop behind the low hills to the west and coolness would start setting in. Rhoda would insist that her pa return to his bed then — and that would take a load off his mind.

"Probably somebody you forgot about long ago," he said. "Man can walk around with a hurt chewing at him for years before he finally takes it on himself to do something about it."

Price brushed at his eyes unsteadily. "Reckon there's a plenty of them doing just that. But I never done no man dirt — not the mean, crooked way. Always paid my score, and I never cheated. Maybe was times when I ramrodded my way a little strong, but I was Bible honest about it."

Rhoda appeared, carrying a cup of coffee. She crossed to where Hagerman sat, pressed it into his hands.

"Here, Pa, drink this. *Mamacita* laced it with brandy. Ought to do you good." She frowned, drew back. "You're cold! I think we'd better get you back to your bed."

"In a minute," he said patiently, gulping the coffee. "Ain't seen the sun go down for quite a spell. Kind of like to watch it tonight."

"All right, but soon as it's gone Shawn's to carry you back up stairs."

The rancher handed the empty cup to her. "Just what he'll do. . . . And you be thanking *Mamacita* for me. The coffee tasted real good."

Rhoda studied him for a long breath, her soft, lovely features gentle and strangely stilled. Abruptly she leaned down, kissed him on the forehead.

"I'll tell her, Pa."

Hagerman watched her move off, a distant loneliness in his eyes. Suddenly garrulous, he had been emptying himself and now he was growing tired.

"A fine girl . . . woman," he murmured, after Rhoda had entered the house. "A real looker . . . like her ma only she's got more spunk. Know what I seen her do once? We was in town together, getting something. Don't recollect what. There was this here stranger and he up and says, sort of smart like, to me, 'So you're the big kingpin they call Mr. Texas!'

"Well, sir, she turned on him, slapped him so hard his hair rattled. That's just what she done."

Shawn smiled. He would expect that of Rhoda.

Hagerman brushed at his lips, coughed, swallowed hard. "A real woman, that little gal. . . . You know, I never minded much being called that. Made me kind of proud, in fact. Big, fine country like this and having folks sort of tie me into it, making me a part of it seemed good. Always figured it was kind of a compliment. . . . The sun going down?"

Starbuck glanced to the west. Low hanging clouds had raised the horizon and color was beginning to fill the sky.

"Just about."

"Thought things was changing. Real pretty how the blue gets all sort of filled with gold and the bottoms of the clouds get yellow and sometimes red. Wish't now I'd taken time to watch a little oftener. . . . Same with sunrise. . . ."

The rancher's voice seemed to drag, become fainter. Starbuck stepped up onto the porch, looked closer at Hagerman. He seemed to have shrunk, to have receded deeper into the quilt that now engulfed him. His face was a chalk white oval.

"Expect we'd best be getting you back in bed," Shawn said, and, stepping to the door, called, "Rhoda!"

He froze in that next moment as a voice came to him from the yard, one low and guarded.

"You Hagerman? Price Hagerman?"

22

"That's me!" The rancher's voice, filled with some of its old warlike quality, was surprisingly strong. "Who're you?"

The drawling reply was soft, amused. "Not your best friend for sure."

Shawn, unnoticed in the shadow-filled doorway, spun swiftly, gained the edge of the gallery in a single stride. There was no humor in his tone, only a grimness.

"You're dead if you move — and that's for sure!"

The gunman, still on his horse, was lean and small. He had apparently come in from the lower side of the house, working his way through the brush until he reached the yard. He had chosen his moment well, one when none of the crew were about and he was only a dim shape in the hot stillness of sundown.

"I misdoubt that," he murmured, betraying no concern at Starbuck's unexpected presence.

"What is it?" Rhoda asked, stepping into the open. She halted abruptly, caught up by the tense hush, the poised, coiled figure of Starbuck, the vague outline at the fringe of the chamisa.

"The deal's off," Shawn said, hand hovering above the gun on his hip. "Keep riding."

"Reckon I can't do that. . . . Don't move, lady!"

Rhoda, taking a step toward Price Hagerman,

halted. "Is he —"

Starbuck nodded. From the depths of his chair the rancher said: "You're a mite late. Dave Archer beat you to it."

"You're still breathing." The killer's hat was pulled low on his head and his voice had a muffled timbre, as if he were partly masked.

"Maybe not for long. . . . Mind answering me something? Who was it that hired you?"

"Don't see as it matters none to you, old man."

Only the gunman's head moved as he brought his attention back to Starbuck. "I got to go through you, that it?"

"You do. . . . I'm telling you again to forget it."

"Ain't the way I work, mister," the killer said quietly, and threw himself off the saddle into the close-by brush.

The pistol in his hand blasted through the silence. Starbuck, drawing and lunging to the side, felt the bullet rip through the slack in his shirt sleeve. He squeezed off a shot as he went prone, aiming at the blur in the brush.

"Who was it hired you?" Price Hagerman's high-pitched voice cut through the echoes. "I'm asking you — who was it?"

Shawn lay motionless, weapon leveled at the now unmoving blur. He could hear Rhoda sobbing quietly on the porch but there were no sounds coming from the brush. Somewhere back on the hard pack, in the vicinity of the bunkhouses, boot heels rapped. The crew, attracted by the gunshots, were coming.

Rising slowly to a crouch, finger snug against the trigger of his extended weapon, Shawn edged forward. He reached the brush fringe, straightened. A low sigh slipped from his compressed lips. The gunman's draw had been faster, but his own aim had been truer.

The killer lay flat on his back. A broad stain covered his chest. The corners of his mouth were pulled down and a puzzled, defiant frown was on his narrow face.

"Who . . . the hell . . . are you?" he mumbled.

Starbuck shook his head. Kicking out he dislodged the pistol from the gunman's lax fingers, sent it skittering off into the brush. Voices were shouting questions in the yard, overriding the thudding of running boots, and somewhere near the cook-shack one of the dogs had set up a frantic barking.

He turned away, paused, a tall lean shape in the fading light, momentarily stilled by the fact of death at his own hand, and then moved on, stepping up onto the porch where Rhoda was crouched beside Price Hagerman.

The rancher stared up at him from deep-set, filming eyes. "Who . . . he tell you who it was . . . hiring him? Got to know . . ."

Shawn felt Rhoda's glance upon him. He leaned over Hagerman, shook his head. "Didn't catch the name. Was dead before I could get it out of him."

Price stirred weakly. "Sure would like . . . to know."

"No matter," Starbuck replied. "All over with now."

"Yeh . . . reckon so. . . ."

Shawn turned to the men gathered around the dead gunman. "Load him up and take him in to Blackburn. Tell him he's the one we've all been waiting for."

He came back around. Rhoda was tucking the quilt around her father. "He's ready," she said, stepping back. "I don't want him to get cold."

Starbuck gathered the rancher into his arms, hesitated, looked closely into the man's face. A peacefulness had come over it. His half-closed eyes were unseeing. . . . It wouldn't make any difference to Price Hagerman. He would never again feel the cold, the heat or anything else.

Dodge City — that's where Jim Winfield was going, Ron had said.

Starbuck, lashing down his blanket roll to the saddle, paused, stared out over the flat lying north of Hash Knife. . . . Dodge was a long way off. He heaved a sigh, finished with the tarped bedding, and brushed at the sweat collected on his brow. It would be a hot ride, too, but it didn't matter — nothing did if the trail, even though cold, led eventually to Ben. Sometimes, however, the burden of the search grew a bit heavy and the failures discouraging.

It would be easy to quit, to accept one of the offers being made to him, as here at Hagerman's, and forget about his brother and Muskingum and old Hiram's legacy. Hell, he would have ten times the amount coming to him if he would stay on at Hash Knife, become a member of the family. Such would be easy to do, and the refusal became more difficult each time he looked at Rhoda standing nearby, hopeful, waiting.

But it wouldn't be right. Ben, wherever he was, could be finding life less generous; he could be in dire need of his share of the Starbuck estate, and if he quit now, permitted the money to be forever lost, Shawn knew the knowledge of what he had done would haunt him for all time to come. . . . It was the same old story; finding Ben came first, his own needs and desires must wait.

Gripping the sorrel's headstall in his hand, he glanced about the yard. Ron had said his good-bye and thanks, was already on the range. He had taken over as Price Hagerman had always wished and finally admitted that he could. The rancher had died contentedly with that knowledge in his mind.

Only Rhoda remained.

He led the gelding up to the porch, halted, his sober gaze on the girl who stood quietly looking down at him.

"I had hoped you'd change your plans," she said, her voice low and wistful.

He nodded. "A thing I'd do — if I could."

"Maybe you'll find Ben in Dodge. If you do . . . will you come back?"

Shawn reached a hand to her, drew her off the porch to his side. No woman he'd ever met had stirred him as deeply as did this Rhoda Hagerman.

"Plans — promises — they're something I can't afford. All I can say is that I'd like to."

"With Pa gone —"

"I know, but you'll do fine . . . you and Ron. And Hash Knife will get bigger, if that's what you want."

She looked down. "Not what I want, Shawn. I . . . I want you."

He grinned at the frankness of her, at the boldness of her words. But that was Rhoda, an honest chip off old Price Hagerman, and he'd not expected her to be any other way.

"I feel the same toward you, but it's not in the cards. Someday . . . maybe."

"Will you come then?"

"Could be years —"

The girl shook her head. "It won't matter. Hash Knife will be there, and so will I . . . waiting."

"No," he said firmly, almost roughly. "Don't do that. Don't waste your life."

Leaning over he kissed her lightly on the lips, wheeled and swung onto the sorrel. Touching the big red horse with his spurs, he moved out of the yard, holding his eyes straight ahead. When he reached the first rise he looked back. She was still standing at the corner of the house.

Raising his hand in a final salute, Starbuck rode on.

The employees of G.K. Hall hope you have enjoyed this Large Print book. All our Large Print titles are designed for easy reading, and all our books are made to last. Other G.K. Hall books are available at your library, through selected bookstores, or directly from us.

For information about titles, please call:

(800) 257-5157

To share your comments, please write:

Publisher
G.K. Hall & Co.
P.O. Box 159
Thorndike, ME 04986